## ALSO BY LARRY B. GILDERSLEEVE

www.larrygildersleeve.com

*Blue by You*

*The Girl on the Bench*

*Follow Your Dreams*

*Dancing Alone Without Music*

# For the Love of
# Charley Chaplain

# for the
## LOVE OF *Charley* Chaplain

## LARRY B. GILDERSLEEVE
### award winning author of *Blue by You*

*For the Love of Charley Chaplain*

© 2025 by Larry Gildersleeve

Editors: Deborah Froese
Cover and Interior Design: Emma Elzinga

Indigo River Publishing
3 West Garden Street, Ste. 718
Pensacola, FL 32502
www.indigoriverpublishing.com

Ordering Information:

Quantity Sales: Special discounts are available on quantity purchases by corporations, associations, and others. For details, contact the publisher at the address above.

Orders by US trade bookstores and wholesalers: Please contact the publisher at the address above.

Printed in the United States of America

Library of Congress Control Number: 2025916253
ISBN: 978-1-964686-71-4 (paperback)   978-1-964686-72-1 (ebook)

First Edition

*With Indigo River Publishing, you can always expect great books, strong voices, and meaningful messages. Most importantly, you'll always find . . .*
words worth reading.

*The late Reverend Charles E. Flener, known among his law enforcement colleagues as Charlie Chaplain, inspired this fictional book.*

*A dear departed friend whose memory will always be with me.*

# 1

# *Opening Act*

*"There is no agony like having an untold story inside you."*
– Truman Capote

Seabirds circled lazily overhead, silhouetted against overcast skies on a cold and dreary late-February afternoon. Seasonal gloomy weather outside failed to dampen spirits of those gathered inside the boutique hotel a stone's throw from Pike Place Market, a sprawling, century-old downtown venue regarded by many as the soul of Seattle.

Chandelier lights in the opulent ballroom flickered a warning before dimming as latecomers vied for the few remaining seats. Her ceremonial task completed, the presenter of the highly coveted Lanneau Prize for journalistic excellence stepped away, leaving the recipient, Charlene Tuell, a woman many in the audience knew as Charley Chaplain, standing all alone center-stage. The room fell pin-drop silent, all eyes on the beautiful, impeccably dressed woman.

"I was asked to keep my remarks to around twenty minutes. I assure you that won't be a problem. I'll be done in about half that time."

A sudden realization she'd forgotten to thank the articulate em-cee or offer a greeting to attendees added to nervousness already seeping into her voice. She silently prayed for a more relaxed rhythm.

"I've read our world is full of people whose stories must be shared. Never thought mine was one of them." Her hands re-laxed their white-knuckled podium grip. "At first, David agreed. He changed his mind, and despite his charm, something he had in abundance, I remained steadfast. We were at an impasse. Then something happened."

She tilted the microphone up and pulled it closer.

"What happened was David got a different yes than he'd asked for, and all of us are here today because of him. It should be David Jacobs standing before you, not me." Her eyes filled, her hands held fast to the lectern. "Oh, if only he could."

A gust of wind parted low-hanging clouds; sunlight spilled in through windows and skylights; dust particles danced in the sun-beams. Rays of sunshine quickly disappeared as clouds reap-peared. Charlene thought she saw someone standing alone in the shadows beneath the balcony at the back of the room. She looked again. Nothing.

Seconds ticked by. A ringing cell phone and scolding looks cast toward the unwelcome sound brought her back into the moment.

"We had barely eight days together before fate intervened, as fate so often does, and we were forever separated."

She forced her shoulders back and drew a relaxing breath.

"David wrote *"Hearts Beneath Their Shields"* after we parted. Had we known what lay ahead, would we have done things differently? A question I've been asked many times before, and my answer has always been no. No, we would not."

Her downcast eyes studied her notes.

"As it says in Scripture: 'How do you know what will happen to-morrow? For your life is like the morning fog. It's here a little while, then it's gone.'"

She reached for the water glass and waited patiently when the loud chiming of a second phone caused some to look around, others to fidget on their chairs and utter sighs of annoyance.

"On the last day I saw David, control of my life was seized by others for many months. I was taken to a place you'd never want to be. In one of my darkest moments, sitting in that tiny shared jail cell, I was lifted up by the realization God sometimes has a sense of humor when placing people, as well as opportunities and obstacles, in our path. I believe what happens next is all up to us."

Her eyes scanned the audience. "You may not agree, but I hope and pray you do."

She loosely clasped her hands and rested them on the podium's edge. Unhurried now, she'd found her rhythm.

"Someone once said grief distorts everything, including time. Not for me. Not when David and I were together ever so briefly, and not in my memory of those few days. I've cherished every moment I remember after *our* paths crossed less than a year ago."

She paused. "How did we meet?"

Her cheeks lifted beneath her luminous eyes into what a romance author might describe as a fallen-angel smile.

"Well, for those of you who know me, or have read about me, that's the sense of humor part. It certainly wasn't in church."

# 2

# A Chance Encounter

A popular neighborhood bar and a fine dining restaurant filled the ground floor of a two-story, sandstone and brick building on the historic Bowling Green town square in Kentucky's third-largest city. Different owners, separate sidewalk entrances, a connecting passageway. JAR's Pub shared a kitchen with Main Fare and offered a limited menu inside as well as for those seated outside at a half dozen cast-iron, four-top tables.

Under the streetlights, the pavement glistened from an afternoon downpour. Darkened skies and heavy air threatened more. A welcoming neon sign flashed on and off above the weathered, dark-green canvas awning covering JAR's entrance. It caught the attention of a passerby with no other destination in mind.

Lured inside, he lingered for a moment, then ambled left toward the ten-stool mahogany bar that extended a third the length of the room. Nestled against the opposite wall were five wooden booths. Scattered tables and chairs could seat another twenty patrons. At seven o'clock on a slow Thursday evening in early April, with only one booth and two tables occupied, the room felt both intimate and comfortably spacious.

At the far end of the bar, her back to the door, sat a woman whose aloneness could inspire a country music ballad. Well and truly within herself, she didn't sense the new arrival until he was seated several stools away.

After ordering a Knob Creek neat, the man's eyes were drawn toward an ethereal image in the mirror behind the bar. He gazed at the woman's reflection with the same detachment he would an uninspiring museum painting. Or thought he did.

His bourbon arrived, accompanied by the bartender's fingers grazing across the back of his hand. Her eyes conveyed she had more in mind than serving drinks. She drifted away when he didn't respond as she'd hoped.

The reflection took a genteel sip of her drink.

The man's insouciant museum-gazing failed him. The awkward silence slowly turned them toward each other. He raised his glass. "You look a bit lonely over there."

The woman rolled a half-empty glass between her thumb and fingers, then tipped it his direction.

"As soon as I reach bottom, I'll be leaving." Her voice lacked even the hint of an accent marking her as a local. "But thanks anyway."

The comely, early-forties bartender watched and listened before closing back in like a predatory feline approaching its prey, elbows pressed against the sides of a low-cut blouse. "I can always use a friend."

His head lowered slightly. A long count of *one Mississippi, two Mississippi.*

He lifted his chin, made eye contact, and heard himself say, "This is JAR's bar, right?"

"Yep," she answered. "Pub, actually."

"What's the difference?"

"Well, I guess it's—"

"Never mind."

His mind was on the other woman, but his abruptness caused a pouting face just inches from his own. He continued a less than halfhearted effort. "Are those the owner's initials?"

"I guess so. All anyone ever calls him is Jar." She blinked twice, slowly. "And I'm Shirley."

Were her fawning attention not so clichéd, the unfolding scene might have found its way into his writing. He accepted her extended hand adorned with an assortment of rings and fingernails painted scarlet.

"Nice to meet you," he replied.

He tugged; she held tightly.

"You don't sound like yer from around here. Are you from England?"

Even the most casual observer—and there were none at the moment—would know one woman had an itch in need of scratching. The other, watching silently from her perch, decidedly didn't.

"Australia." He gently freed his hand. "Quite some time ago."

"That's a long way from here," Shirley said.

"It is," he answered dryly.

A well-dressed elderly man, steadied by his ornate cane, entered through the passageway from the restaurant and with slow, deliberate steps, found his way to a stool at the opposite end of the bar. Shirley reluctantly peeled herself away.

The mirrored reflection turned her head slightly, the man from "down under" filling the corner of her eye.

"You *are* a long way from home. Sydney? Melbourne? Brisbane? The Outback, perhaps?"

"Interested?"

"Truthfully, I'm not." She reached for her glass. "Forget it."

He brushed her answer aside and pressed on. "Adelaide. Born

and raised." And on. "Capitol of South Australia, one of seven states." And on. "Everyone's friendly there. Or almost everyone." He sipped his drink. "And in California, where I live now." *One Mississippi, two Mississippi.* "That's all I'm trying to be."

"I see." She averted her eyes. "Well, thank you for that, but I have plenty of friends." She finished what remained of her drink and gave him a sideways glance. "And I long ago reached my quota of troubled ones."

He took a long swallow of his bourbon before he plunged ahead. "That's disappointing. And how, may I ask, does *troubled* look to you?"

She rested her elbow on the bar and pointed a manicured finger with clear nail polish at the male image in the mirror staring back at her.

His mouth curved into a smile. "Clever."

"Glad you think so," she answered, unsmiling.

Nothing she'd said or done offered encouragement, but he had no place else to be, no one else to talk with, and he'd found this kind of sparring with strangers occasionally provided dialogue for movie scripts when his imaginary friends stopped talking to him.

"How did you know?" he asked. "About me and being troubled."

She turned to face him. "I used to be in the trouble business. And believe me, there's nothing casual about how you wear yours."

She was right. He was troubled. Deeply troubled. And he was further troubled it was apparent to a complete stranger sitting far from him in a dimly-light room.

His voice wavered. "I must say, that sounds rather *casually* imprecise."

"Just a messenger."

"By the way, my name is—"

She raised her hand. "No names. Please. And before this goes any further, I'm here to be alone."

8

She'd been to JAR's on a weeknight and envisioned a solitary respite from *her* troubles when she left a friend's house an hour earlier. She sought to stem the flow of unwanted conversation.

"Not interested in any notion of not being alone," she continued. "Here or someplace else you might have in mind."

Undaunted, he sought to keep the dialogue tap open.

"Not interested in not being alone," he repeated with slow weight. "No worries. Alone is fine by me." Long accustomed to a writer's solitary life, he added, "I'm alone a lot myself."

He teased out an exaggerated grimace when she said, "No surprise there." Her tone softened. "Me too. And thank you for understanding."

He lifted his glass, realized it was empty, and set it back down. "You were about to tell me the trouble business you used to be in."

She pushed back yet again. "I think not."

Though she had no interest in continuing verbal volleyball, she found herself appraising the stubborn player on the other side of the net. Even in the bar's stygian setting, his complexion had an unhealthy pallor, and she'd soon understand its incongruency with an otherwise fit-looking, clean-shaven man in his late fifties or early sixties. Early fifties would make them the same age. The beginnings of a receding hairline crept up against his thick brown hair with just a few gray brushstrokes at the temples. A slate-colored cashmere sweater over a white, silk-cotton blend golf shirt. Bare ankles between black jeans with a starched crease and his black, tasseled loafers made from a reptile's skin.

She gave him a six, maybe even a seven, on a lofty ten scale, and couldn't help wondering if some woman in California had influenced his pleasing sense of fashion.

Watching her watching him, he cast aside any misstep regrets and emulated her lack of subtlety. His mind turned to how he would describe her on paper, knowing his written words were often better chosen. He settled on *beautiful in an alluring sort of way*. In days to come, he'd learn his "well-rounded" assessment of her curvaceous figure, small waist above shapely hips, could serve as a metaphor for the life of the woman he hadn't expected to meet until the following morning.

Neither wanted to convey the slightest weakness by asking what the other was thinking.

He served up his question again. "What kind of trouble business?"

She coaxed shoulder-length brunette hair away from her sea-green eyes and sighed heavily before sending the metaphorical ball sailing back over the net.

"The police kind."

He straightened. "You're a cop?"

"Was."

His mind raced. *No way.* Lingering uncertainty led to a hesitant, stumbling reply. "Let's say, for the moment, I believe you."

"Let's say." Her perch had become as uncomfortable as the conversation she sought to escape, and she became incensed at his staring. "What?"

"You don't look the part."

"What part?"

"Well, at the risk of offense, all your parts."

Her penetrating eyes sought his, but not in a kind way.

"It doesn't surprise me Australian men can leer just like Americans. And it shouldn't surprise you I'm offended. As any woman would be." She inclined her head toward Shirley farther down the bar. "Well, perhaps not every woman."

The sting of her reply knocked him back.

"I'm embarrassed. Truly, I am. And I'm sorry." He gamely tried to regain his footing. "But let's be honest. Why should I believe you?"

"About wanting to be left alone?"

"No, no. About you being a cop."

She thought for a moment, then reached into a luxury-brand handbag resting on the empty stool nearest her. A flick of her wrist sent an object sliding smoothly across the shiny surface of the heavily-waxed bar.

He lifted the soft black leather casing, held it for a few seconds, then wedged a thumb into a crevice to open it. His challenge now would be to look and sound surprised as his uncertainty about her identity vanished.

"Long way from home. A police chaplain?"

She shrugged her narrow shoulders, which seemed molded to a light tan, tailored linen jacket covering a buttoned-up white silk blouse tucked into a laurel green skirt.

"If that's what it says, it must be so. Wouldn't you think?" she asked.

He cast a questioning look that invited more.

"Apparently not," she continued. "Okay, then. Ordained. Used to work with the cops. Was one myself." She looked away and ruefully added, "In a former life."

When her daughter, an only child, left for college in California, Charlene Tuell had parlayed her seminary degree into becoming a social worker. After a few years, when she was no longer intimidated by her then-husband's vehement opposition, her volunteer work became a full-time profession.

Assigned to the Charlie Sector (the others Alpha and Baker) in Seattle, her fellow officers, respectfully and with affection, nicknamed her Charley Chaplain. A nod to both the Charlene nickname she'd gone by since childhood and to the famed actor in early twentieth century silent movies.

The combination of her unique career and the catchy sobriquet found its way into feature articles in newspapers, magazines, and broadcast media, locally and regionally. She never became comfortable with the public relations notoriety the police department encouraged and obligated her to endure.

All that was now in her life's rear-view mirror.

The Australian carefully closed the bi-fold case containing a gleaming silver Seattle Police Department shield. He moved off his stool and leaned across with an outstretched arm toward her waiting hand.

"Then why do you still have it with you?" he asked as she dropped the shield into her purse.

He took a chance sitting with only two empty stools separating them and was pleasantly surprised when his encroachment went unchallenged.

"In case a smile and polite deference aren't enough to avoid a traffic ticket." Her eyes found his. "And to discourage . . ." Her voice trailed off.

He was enjoying the back and forth and thought she was as well. "I guess it could thwart a stranger in a bar asking 'your place, or mine?'"

Accustomed to men paying her unwanted attention, she couldn't yet bring herself to leave. "Ya, think?"

"Yep. Guess that could be a little off-putting."

"No, a *lot* off-putting."

After a long silence, he thought of a peace offering.

"Would I be endangering my life if I offered to buy you a drink?" He tapped a finger on the top of his glass. "I'm thinking of having another, and it's still early."

"No."

He knowingly risked agitating her even further. "Are you referring to my life being imperiled or my offer of another drink?"

"Both."

"I see. We're not getting on very well, are we?" Like a skilled trial attorney who only asks questions in court to which the answer is already known, he was emboldened by knowing who she was. "Everyone has a story, and I'll bet yours is really something. Care to share?"

"I'll save it for the person I'm meeting." She hesitated. "Or not."

He also hesitated before deciding against revealing *he* was that person.

"That's odd."

"In what way?" she asked.

"You said earlier you came here to be alone."

"And truth-telling is what you expect in a bar?"

"Well said." He looked at his watch. "I have no place to be. I can warm this stool 'til he arrives. I doubt they'll ask us to leave if we only have one drink."

"You assume I'm here to meet a man."

"A fair assumption, I think. But okay, until he or *she* arrives."

"You assume my meeting is tonight," she continued.

"It isn't?"

His question went unanswered. Being with her was a welcome distraction from, as she'd said earlier, the trouble he was wearing not so casually. Despite his best efforts, he sensed their conversation coming to an end when she eyed the door through which they'd both entered.

"It would appear I'm meeting myself coming and going," he said, "and getting nowhere."

"And now it is I who must be *getting going*." She slid effortlessly off her stool, reached into her purse for her wallet, and withdrew a single bill. She caught the bartender's eye. "Both of us."

He watched as she laid the bill next to her empty glass and turned to walk past him.

"A fifty? You've either been here a long time or you're extremely generous."

"Consider it my treat. For you"—she angled her head toward the far end of the bar—"and your new friend. I have no doubt I've disappointed you. She might be more to your liking."

"Don't know what you mean," he answered innocently.

"Oh, come now. We both know she has something other than idle chit-chat in mind." She moved a few steps away, stopped, turned around. "Russell Allen Wilson."

"Who's Russell Allen Wilson?"

"The owner."

He furrowed his brow in a meditative moment. "That would make this, what, the RAW Bar? So where did JAR come from?"

"Some other time."

"Some other time. For you and me? That sounds promising."

An *in your dreams* look accompanied her parting words. "Doubtful. Enjoy the rest of your evening."

He wasn't alone in watching her gracefully navigate between the scattered tables and chairs, some now occupied. One man, sitting alone, set down his beer and signaled to no one in particular a two-thumbs-up rating of the woman who'd just departed.

David watched Shirley pick up the empty glass streaked with a trace of lipstick and a crisp, green portrait of Ulysses S. Grant.

"She said she was buyin' for both of you. Want another?"

"No, thanks."

"Couldn't help hearing some of that. Didn't go well, did it?"

He eyed the door. "Maybe yes, maybe no."

"Maybe rain, maybe snow."

"What?"

"Oh, just somethin' my gramma used ta say."

He rose from his stool and started to walk away.

"Will you be coming back again sometime?" she asked hopefully.

He turned and echoed the now-departed reflection. "Doubtful." He paused and added pleasantly, "Shirley, it was nice meeting you."

14

Moisture dripped from JAR's frayed awning when he stepped out into the misty evening air. He looked both directions and found himself in a crowd of one. In the stillness, he heard the distant whistle of an approaching freight train continuing its southern passage. He looked across the street to lights illuminating the still-wet leaves on towering magnolia trees in Fountain Square Park.

*That was quite something*, he thought, smiling. The morning's promise lightened his step as he dodged rain puddles on his way back to a nearby hotel.

# 3

# Not What I Expected

The storm moved through during the night. An hour or so after a cloudless spring sunrise, the former chaplain was seated in a booth at a noisy comfort food diner in a part of town whose best days were decades past. The venue hadn't been of her choosing. As delicately as possible, she held a laminated menu tacky from syrup and who knows what else. She sensed another's presence.

"It's you. *Again*." She dropped the menu, and with sharpness in her voice as crisp as the corners of an envelope, asked accusingly, "Stalking me?"

He wasn't surprised by her reaction, her words, or the unpleasant glint overtaking her eyes. This morning, he knew he'd have the upper hand, once he got past the frost line. He pointed to a large purse on the bench.

"No need to reach for your kryptonite shield," he answered affably. "It's a short stack of blueberry pancakes I'm stalking. Told the best in town can be found here. Saw you when I came in." He paused for her to speak. She didn't. "May I join you?"

She noticed his sweater and jeans selections were different from the night before, and that smooth and tasseled burgundy loafers had replaced reptilian ones. Socks still missing. She rolled her sticky fingertips across her thumbs, careful not to touch her white cable knit sweater or designer blue jeans.

Intent on keeping him at bay, she surveyed the room. "I'm meeting someone."

"You said that last night."

"True then. True now," she replied evenly. *What's it going to take to get through to him?*

She wiped her hands with a paper towel plucked from the upright stand on the table. She hoped he'd just leave her alone but didn't expect he would.

He noticed four women at the table nearest them had stopped their conversation. He assumed they anticipated something far more interesting than gardening, grandchildren, and the shortcomings of their husbands. He stepped to his right to block their prying eyes, leaned in, and lowered his voice. "What time?"

"Eight."

"You're quite early," he whispered, "and I was wondering if I might—"

She'd also noticed the eavesdropping women and made sure they could hear her response: "Asked and answered."

Four words or less in each of the six times she'd spoken.

"You know, there's no need to be this way," he answered quietly but firmly. He straightened up. "It's unnecessary and if I may say, unbecoming."

She lowered her voice to match his, her words blending pique with defensiveness. "Well, how's *that* for putting me in my place?"

He replied, "Sorry," but wasn't. He would have walked away save for a promise he'd made to a friend, now wishing he hadn't. He canvassed the restaurant.

"There still aren't any open tables. May I at least join you for a cup of coffee? I'll leave as soon as your friend arrives. Promise."

She looked around absently. Discolored walls. A mix of linoleum and ancient hardwood floors beneath unmatched tables and chairs. An overall décor reminiscent of a lower-end consignment store.

"It's not a trick question," he gently prodded.

*Perhaps I've misjudged him.*

Several more seconds passed before she offered a welcoming gesture. Of sorts.

He took his place across from her. "Thank you."

She fixed a stern look toward the women inviting them to mind their own business, and was rewarded with chagrined faces. She turned her attention to the man sitting much closer to her than the night before. "I'll say this for you, Mr. Australia. You're nothing if not tenacious."

An opening for him to play fair and level the playing field by divulging his name.

Before he could respond, a waitress about the same age as Shirley but looking nothing at all like her, appeared. She dispensed coffee, then pulled an order pad from her wrinkled apron and a pencil from behind her ear.

He thumbed at himself. "Together."

Things were progressing much faster than the chaplain could have anticipated. "Separate."

He grinned, as did the waitress as she took their orders, gathered up menus, and left. His grin twisted into an amused smile.

"Cozy, isn't it?"

She slowly creamed her coffee, and a conciliatory tone wrapped around her words. "Please tell me you're not talking about us."

*A thawing, perhaps?* "No, ma'am. This place."

Although the town had grown in a different direction over the years, as far back as the late 1960s, locals knew Karen's Kastle as *the*

19

place for comfort food and respectful conversation. In the large window by the entrance, hand-drawn by Karen Thurman in bold letters on a wrinkled sheet of butcher's paper, was an impossible-to-miss framed greeting: *Be Nice or Leave, Thank You.* It had been there as long as anyone could recall. Failure to comply—and it happened from time to time—caused the offender upon departing to be invited nicely not to return.

Karen's Kastle was open for breakfast and lunch, and those who crossed the threshold came from all walks of life. It was not uncommon for the clientele to offer quiet blessings at their tables before eating, and in the thematic Kings and Queens restrooms hung signs admonishing *Wash your hands & say your prayers 'cuz Jesus 'n germs are everywhere.*

Each time the ancient cash register rang loudly, Karen wished her customers "Have a blessed day" to send them properly on their way. If Karen could have *her* way, Sunday morning churches wouldn't still be the most segregated gathering places in America.

The tense quiet in their booth contrasted with conversations varying in loudness and animation all around them. Each waited for the other to speak.

Curious how things would play out, he decided to wait to introduce himself. "Don't think I said good morning. I apologize. Good morning."

She lowered her coffee cup. Her lips compressed into a thin smile, and a bit of color crept into her cheeks. "Good morning to you."

"Here's a thought. Until your friend arrives, we could revisit last night."

"Let's not," she replied.

"As I recall, we left off with me asking you to tell your story and—"

"I can see your listening skills haven't improved overnight," she interrupted, though not unpleasantly.

"Okay, then. To pass the time until you send me away, how 'bout I tell you my story?"

She shook her head with exaggerated slowness.

"We've got to talk about something." He feigned inspiration. "I know. What if I share just my 'today' story?"

"Fine, I guess." Beginning to enjoy his company despite her reservations, she leaned forward slightly. "Did you get up early?"

"I did," he replied, puzzled. "Why do you ask?"

She struggled not to smile. "Oh, just trying to get a feel for how long your 'today' story will take."

"Good one." He creased a paper towel. "And now your secret's out."

She leveled her eyes and cautiously asked, "What secret?"

"Tough on the outside, tender on the inside." He sipped his coffee. "Clever, too."

She relaxed. "A bit over the top, don't you think? Especially for this early in the morning."

He thought a shrug-enhanced smile was a sufficient reply.

"And what about you? Could be wrong, but it seems to me your idea of conversation is more akin to scripting a stage play."

"Who knows?" He raised his eyebrows. "Maybe I am."

Breakfast arrived, and he tucked in the paper towel like a cravat. He'd ordered one of several Kastle specials: pancakes, eggs over-easy, crisp bacon, homemade buttermilk biscuits, grits, hash browns, and freshly squeezed orange juice. Her taken-by-surprise lack of interest had spawned a dismissive "I'll have the same" to the waitress, and now there was food plentiful enough for at least four spreading across the Formica table.

She started to ask about his "maybe" remark, but he was talking again.

"For the longest time, I've dreamed of owning a new Corvette and—"

"Forgive me, but we may only have time for your 'today' story."

He continued, undeterred. "All Corvettes are made here. In just a little while, I have an appointment to walk the assembly line and watch them put the finishing touches on mine."

As she listened, she contemplated how best to attack the largesse before her. Knife and fork in hand, she attempted carving the mountain of food into something manageable. She wondered if she'd even like blueberry pancakes.

When she noticed his left hand in a relaxed, half-closed fist on the table between two plates, she set her knife aside and carefully reached across to touch it with the fingertips of her right hand. "And this memorable experience is why you're here instead of just having the car shipped to wherever you live in California?"

He hoped her casual, non-flirtatious gesture meant the frost was melting away. "California. You remembered from last night. Don't know if you want me to be, but I'm encouraged."

She again suppressed a smile, something becoming increasingly difficult. "If you're thinking what I think you may be thinking, don't be."

Her expression didn't offer a clue if she was teasing or not, and although she didn't continue, she didn't pull her hand away. Eating became secondary to conversation.

"Anyway, to answer your question, the car is also a means to an end. Driving Route 66, all the way from Chicago to Santa Monica. Another dream of mine." He thought anyone would interrupt. She didn't. "Do you know about America's Highway?"

"Very little." She moved her hand to her coffee cup. "And you're doing all this now, the car and the trip at the same time, before the clock runs out and old Father Time catches up with you. That it?"

He pressed his lips together tightly. He remembered her saying something the night before about nothing casual in how he wore his trouble. *Where had her remark come from?* Only he, his doctors, and Mac knew his trouble. Knew how precarious his life had become.

"You might say so," he finally answered.

They ate mostly in silence, reflecting on where they'd found themselves on a springtime Saturday morning. One thought it was accidental; the other knew it wasn't.

"I understand. About the car and the trip. And good for you." She felt he was searching her face for sincerity. "I'm being serious. Really, I am." She was relieved when he appeared satisfied. "Curious about one thing, though."

He waited, then asked wordlessly with an upraised open palm.

"I get the whole Corvette thing. Male baby boomer aspiration. You've added, as I understand it, the lure of the open road and all that goes with that."

"True."

"Then how'd you come to be enamored of Route 66?"

"Because I'm Australian?"

She'd just taken a bite of pancake; her reply was a curt nod.

"Been here a long time. Long enough to become Americanized." He paused. "Sort of."

"And?"

"My friend inspired me. He'd made the drive once. Talked about it often."

She waited. Nothing more. They continued eating.

"Does your inspiring friend have a name?"

"Jim."

She tilted her head while knowingly taking the bait. "I see. Is his last name a secret?"

"McKenzie. Jim McKenzie. Likes folks to call him Mac and most everyone does. Used to live up the highway in Louisville. Great guy. He and I—"

He stopped when he saw the fingers that had so recently touched his hand pull at the cuff of her long-sleeved sweater to expose a gold Cartier tank watch.

"You've got about ten grand there on your wrist. Give or take. Standard police issue in Seattle?"

"Of course not." She pulled her sleeve down. "Some people think mine is the fruit of a poisonous tree."

"I don't understand."

"I hope you never will."

He looked around the café. "Have you been stood up again?"

"Again?"

"Last night."

"Oh, that." She bowed her head and studied her napkin. "Well, this morning I really *was* expecting to meet someone."

"You don't appear upset."

She looked up. "I'm not. Relieved, in fact."

"In that case, we now have time for my whole story. Then yours."

"I don't mean to be unkind. Really, I don't. I should be on my way."

"Can't say I didn't offer. A couple of times."

"And a kind offer it was."

Appetites satiated, their meals were far from half-eaten. A Kastle trademark. More, often much more, is better. And if you leave hungry, Karen knew you didn't try hard enough.

She reached for her purse. He picked up both checks. She started to object.

"Last night you treated me. My turn."

"Thank you. That's very kind." She slid toward the edge of the bench. "And now I must be going."

They still hadn't exchanged names. *Remarkable*, he thought, *but fixable.*

"One thing. Before you go."

Her inquisitive look and the setting down of her satchel beckoned him to continue.

"A woman police chaplain, all the—"

"Former chaplain."

"A *beautiful* former police chaplain all the way from the Left Coast, sitting alone last night in a bar in Kentucky . . ."

She smiled. "Thank you for that. And—"

". . . could be the makings of a novel . . . if one gives imagination full reign."

"What makes you say that?" She recalled her stage play comment. "Are you a writer?"

"I've been trying to tell my story."

"So, you are?"

An obedient nod. "Screenwriter. And since you haven't asked, I live where I work. Hollywood."

Recognition lit up her eyes much like a switched-on light illuminates a darkened room.

"It can't be! *You're* the writer Marla Jo Taylor wanted me to meet here this morning?"

"What are the odds, huh? But yes. And I have qualities that go way beyond that label."

Her eyes still wide, she struggled with the unexpected. "I'm sure you do. But why didn't you say something when you first sat down? Or last night?"

"Last night, you said no names. Remember?"

"What'd you expect? Thought you were a stranger on the make. Never imagined you were, well, you." She shook her head. "Not at all what I expected."

"Well, I'm with you there. You're not at all what I expected."

She hurriedly asked, "And how is it I'm less than you expected?"

"Didn't say less."

"Different?" she asked, retreating.

25

"I'll say. Last night I stepped all over myself commenting on your parts. Remember?"

A faint blush of embarrassment colored her neck.

He carefully reached across the cluttered table. "I'm David. David Jacobs."

She slipped her hand into his. "And I'm Charley. But I'm guessing you knew that in the bar."

"Not right away. But yeah, the shield was a bit of a clue. And coincidence out of the question."

"Understood. By the way, that's with an *e-y*, not *i-e*."

"I know. Marla Jo coached me. Nice to meet you, Charley with an e-y Chaplain."

"And you as well," she answered. "I think."

"First impressions can be wrong. Mine about you certainly were. And I'm willing to wager I'm not the first."

"True. I've found judging someone is easy. Getting it right? Not so easy."

"How've you dealt with people misjudging you?"

She lowered her eyes. "Usually found a way to work it to my advantage."

"I'm sure you did. If I may ask, how did that work?"

Her eyes found his. "I could quote you chapter and verse of Scripture until closing time. Would that help?"

"Perhaps, but I'd rather you didn't."

"Not a Christian?"

He removed his paper towel cravat and set it on the bench beside him. "You could say that. And you'd be right."

All conversation in the diner ceased as dishes and flatware clattered noisily to the linoleum floor when a nearby diner stepped out of his booth and collided with a waitress carrying an over-laden tray.

Charley used the distraction to collect her thoughts.

"We're here because my friend Kristi has a big mouth. About

me, that is. She talked to her friend Marla Jo, who turns out to also be your friend, and—"

Their waitress passed by. David handed her the checks and a fifty-dollar bill. "Keep the change."

Effusive would best describe the waitress's gratitude before departing.

"I'll repeat what you said last night. Isn't that a bit generous?"

"As I struggle to match wits with you, Charley, at least allow me to try and match tips."

"Fair enough," she replied with a bemused smile. "And you came all the way from sunny California to talk about writing a book about me. I guess I should be flattered. No, I *am* flattered."

"The truth is, I was coming here anyway. I suspect my plans were set before yours."

She thought for a moment, then playfully slapped her forehead. "That's right. Your car."

"You got it. Anyway, Marla Jo *is* a friend, as you say. We've worked together on some writing things over the years. As to what she told me about you . . . next to nothing."

In truth, Marla Jo Taylor and David Jacobs had talked in the early afternoon the day before. David knew a great deal about Charlene Tuell before their chance encounter in the bar. But then, and now, he wanted to hear her story from her.

"But you heard enough you agreed to write a book about me?"

"Nope. Not even close. But let me ask. Other than your clever moniker in a title, why did *you* agree?"

When a literary agent approached her about sharing her story, Charley initially warmed to the idea of writing an inspirational non-fiction book based on her unique career and notoriety. She talked it over with Kristi Andrews, her best friend in Seattle, who believed it might be just the ticket to get Charley healthy again, mentally and emotionally. And Kristi thought a successful book might have the added benefit of exacting a measure of revenge on Charley's ex-husband.

Kristi had taken it upon herself to advance the idea to Marla Jo Taylor, a college classmate and successful writer living in Kentucky. Marlo Jo's husband, Ben, remembered reading about "Charley Chaplain" in a Seattle newspaper while visiting there years ago. He agreed a book might have promise, adding another voice to those urging Charley onward. But on the nonstop flight from Seattle to Nashville, the closest major airport to Bowling Green, she'd made her decision.

"I haven't agreed. And I won't. I promised Kristi I'd listen to Marla Jo. I did. I promised Marla Jo I'd meet you. Now I have. Done and done. All that's left now is for you and me to go our separate ways, back to our separate lives."

He stared into his empty coffee cup. "If that's what you want."

"Don't you?"

He lifted his eyes to meet hers. "I thought we might try to be more than just friends."

"Wouldn't we first have to become friends?"

"Getting ahead of myself."

"Just a wee bit."

He smiled. "Happens from time to time. So, what about being friends?"

She let his words marinate, thinking about his assertion he had qualities beyond being a writer. From their brief time together over the past twelve hours, she had no doubts. Her doubts were about herself.

"Not much future in that, wouldn't you think? You off on Route 66, back to California."

"True. What about you?"

She sought a place on the crowded table to rest her empty hands.

Finding none, she dropped them to her lap.

"Here for a while, then probably back to Seattle." She knew she had to return, though not as quickly as she'd soon learn.

"On the other hand—"

"Is there one?" she asked.

"I think so. Go with me now to watch my car being born. Have dinner with me tonight. You might even come to like me." With a sheepish grin, he added, "Just a *wee* bit."

Her face broke into an unrestrained smile.

"I might, at that. I just might. But I'll pass on the car birthing."

"Why?"

She reflected for a few seconds. "Too much of an intimate experience for you to be sharing with someone you barely know."

He couldn't mask his disappointment." Any chance I can persuade you it isn't?"

She shook her head.

"Okay, for dinner, how about—"

"I didn't say yes to that either."

He hoped she was only being coy. "Well?"

"Sure, why not," she answered matter-of-factly with a shrug. "I have nothing else planned."

"It's not an act of mercy. It's just dinner."

"Sorry, David." Concern in her voice. "Didn't mean to come across that way." She looked at his stoic countenance. "Does that mean you don't want to have dinner with me now?"

*One Mississippi, two Mississippi.* "Only kidding. I'll even dress up. Over dinner, we can plan the rest of our weekend."

She was relieved to be back in the game. "Aren't you the confident one?"

"Confident? No. Optimistic? Yes. Should I be?"

"Maybe yes, maybe no."

"Funny. I said that very thing last night, but you were already gone."

"And yet, here we are." She paused. "Mark 9:23."

"I don't understand."

"Biblical shorthand for anything's possible."

After hearing "Have a blessed day" from Karen as they departed her Kastle, Charley and David exchanged cell phone numbers while standing in the oil-stained and uneven gravel parking lot close to nearby railroad tracks. They agreed David would make dinner reservations and pick her up at Marla Jo's house in a leafy, highly desirable suburban neighborhood.

"Should I be on the lookout for your new chariot?"

"Of course," he replied.

"Excited?"

"Beyond words."

"Coming from a Hollywood wordsmith, that's saying something."

"You'll find I often err on the side of understatement."

"Something I already know."

"Thought you might."

A warm smile accompanied, "Until tonight, Mr. Australia."

# 4

# *Maybe Yes, Maybe No*

**D**avid watched the final hour of his car's assembly, then learned it wouldn't be fully prepped for red carpet delivery at the Corvette Museum across from the factory until the next morning. He called Charley.

Her well-chosen words were genuinely empathetic, intended to soothe his disappointment. She knew he could easily walk from his hotel to JAR's Pub and suggested they meet there at six-thirty ahead of the Main Fare dinner reservations he'd made for seven.

David thought about Charley all afternoon and arrived early, only to find her already perched where she'd been when they first met. This time, she was far more relaxed and watched him stroll in.

David's promised "dressing up" meant sporting a cashmere blazer, black with gold buttons, and an unstarched, untucked, high thread-count white cotton shirt. An encore appearance of his black jeans and sockless alligator shoes.

Charley mentally confirmed a solid seven rating, one notch be-low her ex-husband, two below many Hollywood leading men and three below international male models.

He resisted an impulse to greet her with a casual kiss on the cheek as he mounted the stool beside her. "You haven't ordered yet."

"No. Waited for you."

Behind the bar stood a man with a pleasant countenance who looked to be about David's six-foot height, younger but rounder. Much rounder. A fate that often befalls men when their athletic ca-reers end but their sizable appetites remain.

"David Jacobs," Charley said, "meet Russell Wilson. He's the owner."

David shook the proprietor's outstretched hand. "That would be Russell *Allen* Wilson if I recall correctly. My pleasure."

"Mine, as well. Charley told me the two of you were here last night. Sorry I missed you. What're you folks havin'?"

"May I?" David asked.

Charley nodded.

"She'll have a top-shelf bourbon of your choosing . . . with ginger ale. I'll have a Knob Creek neat."

David had an easy sureness about him and a certain restlessness within him that had kept Charley off-balance during their first two encounters. Now, she felt beguiled by it. For his part, he couldn't help noticing the smiles of familiarity Charley and Jar exchanged before he went away.

"I'm impressed. I really am," she said. "You remembered his full name."

"As this morning, you remembered my home is in California."

"Seems we were both somewhat paying attention last night. But how'd you know bourbon and ginger ale? I didn't order while we were together."

"Shirley told me."

"Ah. I see. The bartender. Was that before or after you left together at closing time?

"Nice try. I assure you I took my leave right after you. Alone. But not before asking her what you were drinking."

"In anticipation of tonight?"

"In the hope of tonight."

The net was up. Serve and volley. Drinks arrived, and they touched glasses.

"So," David began, "tell me about Jar. How is it you, ever so far away from home, know his name when his employee didn't?"

"Simple, really. My Seattle friend Kristi, Marla Jo, her husband Ben, and Jar were classmates at the university here. They try to get together every couple of years for some kind of campus event. I met 'em all last year when I tagged along with Kristi."

"And his nickname?"

"Okay, look over at him," she whispered. David cast a discrete glance. "Does his shape remind you of a cookie jar?"

"Well, I guess so. In a way. To whom does he owe the bequeathing?"

"I'm told a high school girlfriend. The name followed him to college; she didn't."

Jar returned with a bowl of nuts and a basket of pretzels. He winked at Charley before taking his leave.

David tried to keep jealousy out of his voice. "I saw that. Something goin' on between you two?"

"Oh, I know he's smitten with me. He's very sweet and kind, but I'm not in the market. Likely never will be again." She turned the conversation toward David. "Tell me about your visit to the maternity ward. Was it all that you hoped for?"

"More."

He studied his drink.

She recalled him saying earlier he often erred on the side of understatement. "And are you going to tell me the more?"

"Saving it for later."

"Well, then. Until later comes, I want you to know I researched Corvettes while you were getting yours. My, my. Can't get a new one for much less than a hundred thousand. Likely a lot more."

"Says the lady with the Cartier watch."

Matching smiles.

"Yeah, I guess in the abstract it seems like a lot, but it's fair dinkum considering I got what I've always wanted."

"Fair dinkum. Is that Corvette boys' club speak?"

"Make fun if you like."

"Oh, I like," she answered with a wide smile.

*She's certainly got a way about her.*

"Australian slang. Slips in from time to time."

"And translated into American, it means . . .?"

"Something that's acceptable. Something worthy."

"Where'd dinkum come from?"

"Looked it up when I was a kid. From Chinese dialect spoken in the gold fields."

They finished their drinks. David paid the tab, shook hands with Jar, and followed Charley through the door leading into Main Fare. As they were escorted to their table, several restaurant patrons noticed them—really, just the radiant Charley. She was, as David had assessed, alluringly beautiful. In his mind, an eight crowding a nine in a matching pearl-gray, wool-blend sweater and modest-length skirt. A small Jerusalem cross dangled at the end of a delicate woven chain.

Their college-age waiter, trying to sound grown-up and worldly, recounted the specials, took their orders, and departed.

Just as he had at Karen's Kastle that morning, David noticed Charley's fingers were unadorned. Marla Jo had told him she was divorced, bitterly so, which partially explained the absence of rings. He'd gotten close himself a couple of times but never made the walk down that aisle. And he hadn't worn a ring after losing his college one while reef diving just weeks after graduation.

"David, I want us to divide tonight's check."

"Out of the question. I invited you."

"I thought it would be *fair dinkum*," she answered, not pausing for him to react. "But all right. And only if I pick up the gratuity."

He smiled and reluctantly nodded consent.

"And speaking of questions," she continued, " I have one for you."

"Ask away."

She hunched forward in her chair and crossed her forearms on the table's edge.

"Who *are* you?"

Her question caught him off-guard. "I introduced myself at breakfast. At least, I thought I did. I'm—"

"I know," she interrupted, leaning back. "I mean the *real* you. In addition to Corvettes, I confess to searching online this afternoon for a Hollywood screenwriter named—"

"David Jacobs."

"Right. And I couldn't find one."

He rested his chin on steepled hands, intending to keep the ball on her side of the net. It worked.

"I know, I know," she said. "My fault for not letting you tell your story. I searched and searched and, well, you don't seem to exist. In the abstract, that is."

"Puzzling, isn't it?"

"At the very least. Unless you're in someone's witness protection program. And I still have ways to find that out."

He sat back and fiddled with his embroidered napkin. "Nothing quite that dramatic. Could've saved you the trouble. Truth is, ever since I moved to Hollywood, and that was a long time ago, no one other than my agent and a few extremely close friends—"

"Like Marla Jo?"

He nodded patiently. "Like Marla Jo. And Mac. They know me

as David Jacobs. Now you."

"And?"

"I write with an assumed name. A nom de plume, as they say."

"Interesting. What is it? Another secret name?"

"It is. Carefully guarded. I might be persuaded to share . . . under the right circumstances." She waited him out.

"But only if we've become friends. Have we?"

She stared back at him.

"Okay. I'm otherwise known as Neville Kay."

"Neville Kay," she repeated. "I like that." She mimed zipping her lips shut. "And I'll keep your secret."

"Thank you."

"Now, with that silliness behind us, I want to hear the rest of your story."

"Let's enjoy our dinners. Save it for dessert."

"As you wish. But I'll hold you to it." She sipped her cocktail. "Anything we shouldn't talk about?"

"I don't know. Politics? Religion?"

"Agreed. I disdain politics. And you've already said you're not a Christian."

"You, on the other hand, have that shiny chaplain's shield."

"I do. And what was it you said last night? Oh yes, no worries. We won't go there."

"No worries? Aussie slang. Hope for you yet."

She raised her glass. He touched it with his.

Dinner conversation ranged far and wide. America's only true sports car that would be his the next day. Their favorite wines—whites for her, reds for him. Books—fiction for her, non-fiction for him (as a respite from his day job). Travel—something he'd done extensively and she hadn't. But nothing in their back and forth revealed anything meaningful about their respective pasts.

Their meals finished and the table cleared, Charley said, "I've been very patient. Time now for you to tell me your—"

Her cell phone vibrated in her purse. "Your story." She glanced at her purse. "Sorry, may I?"

"Of course."

She turned the phone so David could read a text message from Kristi asking her to call. Urgent.

"It's Kristi. She's keeping my dog. Something must have happened."

"Then call you must. Want me to order dessert while you're gone?"

"Thank you, no." She patted her stomach. "Still feeling the effects of Karen's Kastle. Won't be long."

After she left, he swirled the wine in his glass and turned his attention to the white-tablecloth restaurant. A framed glass dividing wall with a brass-encased glass door in the center divided the larger dining area from a smaller room for private parties and overflow. A refurbished corrugated tin ceiling with plantation-style wooden fans and period-perfect antique chandeliers. Deep-pile rust-colored carpeting helped ensure private dinner conversations.

David reflected on his conversation with Marla Jo the day before. She'd told him Charley's parents were deceased, and she had no siblings. Estranged from her daughter, her only child, Charley had no grandchildren and no expectation of any. Her professional calling had recently, and publicly, imploded.

"I'm worried about her. She's a remarkable woman but needs something to give her a purpose in life," Marla Jo had said.

"And you think a book about her is part of the answer?" David replied.

"Ben and I both do. Now that you know some of Charley's story, what do you think?"

"Possibly. But not with me."

"Why?"

"Two reasons. It's not what I do, and I don't have the time."

"That's disappointing. But you'll still meet with her tomorrow morning?"

"I will. But only as a favor to you and Ben." But David admitted to himself he was more than a little intrigued.

After a quick exchange of pleasantries between friends, Kristi told Charley her Seattle attorney was trying to reach her.

"He sounded desperate. Or as desperate as a lawyer can sound, I guess."

"Wonder why?" Charley asked, a sense of foreboding overtaking her.

"Oh, come on! Might it have something to do with you agreeing not to leave the city?" Kristi asked rhetorically. "It was a big risk for you to take, don't ya think?"

"I was only going to be gone a few days. You know I needed to get away."

"Oh, please, Charley. You know how these things work. You were with the cops for a long time. Maybe I'm wrong. Hope I am. Just call your lawyer. And let me know if there's anything I can do until you get back. Oh, make sure to give him your phone number. You gave him mine by mistake."

Charley reached her attorney as he was leaving his office for the weekend at his vacation home, a pleasant ferryboat ride from Pier 52 on the downtown waterfront across Puget Sound to Orcas Island.

Kristi's premonition was well-founded. There was a warrant for Charley's arrest. Her lawyer explained he'd secured leniency to give her time to surrender, but if she wasn't back in Seattle and in custody by the following Friday, a week's time, she'd be a hunted fugitive.

As Charley listened, disbelief quickly morphed into a harbinger of what lay ahead for her in the coming days. The event that had tragically turned her world upside down saddened her each time she thought about it, but never to the point of tears.

## 5

# *Maybe Rain, Maybe Snow*

Her life in free fall after being told of her ex-husband's death, a different Charley returned to the table where David sat waiting. She appeared more like the mirrored reflection David first glimpsed almost exactly twenty-four hours earlier.

He asked about her dog.

"Everything's fine." Her body language betrayed her. Pensive. Distracted. Afraid, even.

"You said no to dessert. How 'bout an espresso, perhaps an Irish coffee?"

"Arsenic on the rocks, if they have it." Worry clouded her face. "With a touch of hemlock."

They sat absorbed in the silence before David stepped into the void.

"Charley, we both know you've just learned something troubling. And, if you'll permit a turn of *your* phrase, there's nothing casual about how you're wearing it."

She managed a wan smile. "There is something, David, but nothing I can talk about now. Nothing for you to do. Thank you for caring. It'll pass with time. That's all I need. Time."

He started to speak; she was quicker.

"Enough of that," she said with a dismissive hand wave. "You were about to tell me your story. I'll help. Begin with Marla Jo. Just getting to know her. She seems like a wonderful woman, someone who could be a true friend."

He acquiesced to the conversational pivot. "She's both. We're writers living half a country apart who occasionally work together. A professional relationship that's turned into a lasting friendship."

In his mind, David had a veritable bank of easily recalled metaphors and analogies he nurtured to populate future writing. He approached a teller's window and withdrew an analogy. "The opposite of, say, Truman Capote and Harper Lee."

"In what way?"

"Know much about them?" he asked. Charley shook her head. "Okay. Childhood friends growing up in a small Alabama town who collaborated professionally as adults. Supposedly, she based her character Dill on him."

"The little boy who was friends with . . . who were they? Oh, yes, Scout and Jem. *To Kill a Mockingbird?*" He nodded. "I loved her book."

"You and tens of millions of others. But, yeah. I've read Capote's jealousy of Harper was well known and that he could be mean-spirited even while she was helping him with his books."

David told her about Harper accompanying Truman to rural Kansas to help research his bestseller, *In Cold Blood.*

"Interesting. And it begs the question: how does Marla Jo help you?"

Straight-faced. "With the big words."

"I'll bet that's not the first time you've written or said that."

"That would be true."

"Okay, then. Since Marla Jo's not here, I'll understand if you don't use big words with me."

He responded with a smile and a tip of his glass.

"Now, David, you promised. What's your story?"

He thought back to his conversation with Marla Jo, and still responded untruthfully. "Asked by someone whose real name I don't know. Doesn't seem fair, somehow. Does it?"

She blinked several times as if each blink required effort.

"And . . .?" he prompted.

"Charlene. Charlene Tuell."

"Like a toolbox?"

"More like *too ill* to go to school." She spelled it for him.

"So, Charley Chaplain is *otherwise known as* Charlene Tuell.

"Clever."

"I thought so," David said. "Make you a deal. About your story and mine."

Grateful to be with someone who, however briefly, enabled distance from painful thoughts of her ex-husband and what awaited her return to Seattle, she answered, "You seem to be holding the cards. Deal away."

He'd had most of the day to think about an idea that came to him during breakfast.

"Instead of telling each other our stories now, we do it while we drive Route 66. We'll have plenty of time. It's a long way to California."

She stared at him as if she'd just awakened from a deep sleep and was trying to orient herself in unfamiliar surroundings.

"I'm sorry. What'd you say?"

He slowly measured his words. "I said. It's a long way to California. Road trip. New car. Leave tomorrow. You and me. Together."

"You're not serious, of course. Just joking around."

He didn't reply.

"Right?"

"Wrong. Couldn't be more serious. I don't just want you to go with me, Charley. I need you."

"Why?"

"To share the driving."

"Where'd this all come from? I mean, you seem like a manly man kinda guy. Why can't you make the trip alone?"

"Looks can be deceiving. Like you being a cop."

"I'll give you that. And . . .?"

"Truth is, I can't do it alone. My friend Mac, I mentioned him before, was supposed to go with me. The day before our flight here, he broke his ankle while playing pickup basketball. Couldn't find anyone else out there on such short notice." He paused. "Then you came along."

Two competing thoughts ricocheted around in her head. The first brought forth an enticing vision of how she could uniquely savor the coming days before losing control of everything in her life. The second was troubling, and she spoke to it first.

"I didn't 'come along' as you say. You pursued me long after the faint of heart would've given up." She paused and studied him. "Something else on your mind besides me being some kind of trip consolation prize?" When he didn't answer, she added, "What happens if I say no?"

David was crestfallen. A look of hopelessness replaced the self-assurance he'd worn so well. "I have no choice but to be in Oregon soon. If you say no, and I hope you won't, I'll ship the car and fly home."

She sensed his disappointment. Maybe, she thought, her doubts about his intentions were misplaced, brought on by anxiety over her own rapidly declining fortunes. She didn't ask about Oregon and stared at him a full fifteen seconds.

She gathered up her purse. "Hold that thought. I'll be back in a minute or two."

David wrongly assumed her destination was the ladies' room.

Charley slipped out the front door and found an unoccupied bench with no one around in front of Barbara Stewart Interiors. Marla Jo answered on the third ring. Charley told her of David's request—his plea, actually—and her concern about fending off unwanted advances.

"If you were me, what would you do?" Charley asked.

"Short and sweet, my dear, short and sweet. In that regard, David can be trusted. Completely. Actually, in any regard. I'd bet my life on it."

"Coming from you, that's beyond comforting."

*But I'll also need to hear it from him. His words. His voice.*

"Charley, what does your heart of hearts tell you?"

"My heart of hearts? Well, fair to say, we haven't been on speaking terms for a while."

Marla Jo knew some of Charley's unsettled life in Seattle. "Well, then, if I may. Two things."

"I'm listening."

"If you have the time and don't go with David, you may come to regret it."

*Time. One of so many things I now don't have.*

"And the second?"

"Ask your heart of hearts if a touch of romance, should it happen with David, isn't long overdue."

"All I'll say for now is there are a lot more shattered pieces to my Humpty Dumpty world than my non-existent love life. I need to get back to David. We can talk tomorrow, so please don't wait up."

David stood and pulled back her chair when she returned. Once they were both seated, he waited for her to speak. It took a while.

"About this trip," she began. "Would it be like Harper traveling to Kansas with Truman?"

"Rolling with the analogy, are we?" he asked tentatively.

"We are."

"Well, given there's no book for us to work on, if we find ourselves in Kansas, unlike the two of them, the two of us will keep going west."

She started to speak, then didn't.

"Something troubling you?" he asked

"Yeah, there is. That part about the two of us."

David thought for a moment. "Are you saying you're worried about me? Like you assumed when we first met?"

"Precisely." She expected a response. She got none. "David, even I know Truman was as gay as springtime. He was known to flaunt it . . . back in the sixties, I think."

"Your point being Harper didn't have to worry. Is that what you're saying?"

She nodded.

He didn't falter.

"Not to worry."

"Huh?"

"You have nothing to worry about."

She'd sought his assurance, yet his few quick words landed on top of her already rock-bottomed self-esteem.

"Are you saying you find me undesirable?"

"No, the opposite. Quite the opposite, in fact."

"Then I don't understand."

David had hoped he'd never have to have this conversation with anyone. But now he felt cornered.

"Charley, things in nature don't always work the way we want.

For some men—sadly, I'm one of them now—finding a woman attractive isn't enough." He started to say more, then stopped. "I hope you understand."

She found his response wanting and grew impatient.

"Do you and Truman Capote have something besides writing in common? Is that what you're saying?"

His demeanor became as stiff as a piano string, and he felt a dryness in his throat. "No, that's certainly not what I'm saying," he answered testily. "I believe I've said enough." He exhaled heavily. "More than enough. We barely know each other."

"My point exactly! This *other* has been asked to travel cross-country with someone she's just met. In a car I'm guessing is so small it'll be hard not to be on top of each other."

He remained quiet.

"But my real concern is the nights."

Without her, there'd be no trip. No dream realized. David's eyes were expressionless, his voice small.

"All I can say is I'm looking for a co-pilot to replace Mac, not a lover. I ask that you take me at my word. And trust me."

She rushed her reply. "If you were me, you'd want you to do better than that."

She'd left him nowhere to hide. He swallowed hard. "All right. Much to my regret, I no longer have lead in my pencil."

Her voice flat, her words deliberate. "I still don't understand."

"I was hoping you would." His eyes found the napkin twisting in his hands. "The truth is . . . medicine I'm taking keeps me from . . . well, rising to the occasion. If you will. That's why, in addition to who I am as a person, I said you have nothing to worry about. And you don't."

She looked away as he looked up. Only a coin toss could determine which of them was more embarrassed.

"Might I ask what medicine? And why?"

"A bunch of different pills." His voice devoid of emotion. "My docs call it a cocktail." He turned his water glass unsteadily in his hand. "Odd characterization, don't ya think?"

He set the glass down. "As for the rest. Benign brain tumor is slowly degrading my eyesight, especially one eye, and affecting my balance. But unlike what you said a few minutes ago about your trouble, time won't heal mine. Things'll get worse. I may even lose the sight in that one eye."

She looked at him with sympathetic eyes and spoke in a sotto voice. "I had no way of knowing,"

"You couldn't have. And not to worry. I've gotten pretty good at fakin' the vision thing and being steady on my feet so others aren't aware. But it's unsafe for me to drive in bad weather. Or any distance at night." A faint smile. "Worse yet, as you can see, the meds have robbed me of my southern California tan."

She thought he was the very picture of human frailty and reached for his hand.

"You said you can't postpone your trip because of something in Oregon. Can't you change whatever that is until your friend Mac or someone else can go with you?"

A world-renowned clinic was the "something." It offered a fragment of hope in treating his tumor. He'd lied to her when he said benign instead of malignant. David had already lost precious months waiting for an opening at the elite facility, and even a day's tardiness meant possible forfeiture to another patient in equally dire straits. He started to explain, then didn't. He wanted her help for a few days, not her pity. The conversation he'd never wanted to have with anyone had already made him feel diminished in her eyes without adding to it.

"The simple answer is no." His shoulders slumped in defeat. "It's a treatment center for my condition. I have to go now, or end up at the back of a long queue of other patients. Been waiting a long time as it is. Don't want to wait any longer."

What she accepted as David's honesty, and his accompanying vulnerability, touched Charley deeply as she grappled with his situation . . . in light of her own.

He had no way of knowing if she was moving his way or not until, still holding his hand, she said, "In these cards you're dealing, going along with you is one thing. Driving your new car is something else entirely." A thoughtful pause. "I could do one, I suppose, but not the other."

David's spirits, and his shoulders, rose with a rush of hope. He thought she was circling a possible yes.

"Is it because it's expensive?" he asked, cautiously.

"And your dream car. Even though I haven't seen it, too much to put on me. Sorry."

"Trust me, Charley," his voice gained confidence, "it's a car like any other. You'll see."

"Put me down as not trusting you on that. How long will this little odyssey of yours take?"

"There won't be time for sightseeing along the way. You need to know that. If we share the driving, it will probably take five or six days, all told. Maybe eight or ten, if we don't. Either way, I can make it work and get to Oregon in time."

While David sensed sunshine behind the dark clouds of his misfortune, Charley's troubles came tumbling back to her with extraordinary clarity. She withdrew her hand. What might work for him wouldn't work for her. If she missed her Friday deadline, they wouldn't sit idly by waiting for her to appear whenever the spirit moved her. She had to turn him down before turning herself in.

Still, the moment didn't seem right.

"Leaving tomorrow?" she asked.

"Yes. And on Route 66 beginning Sunday. Oh, my deal with Mac was that I'd pay all expenses. Same for you."

Reaching for ways to stretch out the conversation, instead of asking what lay in store for him in Oregon, a place she wasn't going anyway, she asked, "Shoe-string budget or deep pockets?"

"Only the best of everything. I promise."

"Will I be hearing more Australian slang?"

"Yeah, nah."

"Which means?"

"Maybe. It means maybe. Now, about our trip. Tomorrow, I'd like for us to leave—"

"You know, if I were to look for the words *presumptuous* and *persistent* in the dictionary, there's a better than even chance I'd see a picture of a presumptuously persistent David Jacobs beside each."

"Good on ya. And I assume your alliteration also applies to Neville Kay."

Uncertainty hung in the air like a smothering blanket as they stood on the sidewalk in front of Main Fare. Charley knew her answer, but looking at David under the hazy streetlight, she couldn't put the words together. An imagined obligation to a friend offered a cowardly way out.

"I know you need an answer," she began, "but tonight, in your words, it has to be *yeah, nah*." Although he smiled, she could easily sense his disappointment. "Marla Jo may be waiting up for me, so I need to get going. I'll call you in the morning."

"I understand. A lot to consider. Won't get much sleep tonight."

"Doubt if I will, either."

"If that's the case, and your answer's the one I'm hoping for, we can leave as soon as we pick up my car. I'll drive. You can sleep."

"We'll see."

She felt a crushing weight of regret as she started to walk away from someone she had no reason to believe she'd ever see again.

"Charley, I need to ask."

She turned. "Yes?"

"Does your hesitancy have anything at all to do with me not being a Christian?"

Among all the many variables she'd had rolling around in her mind like marbles in a cloth bag, this had not been one.

"No. Of course not. Absolutely not. What makes you say that?"

"Simple. We both know none of what I want will happen without you. If that's what's bothering you, I'd hate for unspoken words to be how things end for us."

"Well, even though it has nothing to do with my going or not going, you won't be surprised I've been wondering. But you're right. I wasn't going to ask."

Uncertain about what the next day would bring, he brushed a soft kiss against her cheek.

"Because, Charley," he whispered, "I'm Jewish."

# 6

## *Looking Back*

The premise of a book neither wanted had brought them together. What transpired after their paths first crossed kept them up
well into the early morning hours . . . as they'd both anticipated.

Minutes after leaving the town square, Charley stood under the
front porch light at the Taylor residence. She turned the knob and
pushed open the door. Marla Jo was reading a book in the living
room and, with one look, could tell the evening had exacted a toll on
her houseguest. She took a distraught Charley by the arm, guided
her to one of four saddle-style stools at the kitchen's center island,
and poured them each a brandy.

At her host's invitation, Charley replayed as much as she could
easily recall of her conversations with David and the lawyer's
phone call.

Marla Jo listened to the other woman's fears, doubts, and conflicted feelings, then reached to take Charley's hands in hers.

"Must have been a very trying evening. What are you going to
tell David when you call?"

"I have no choice but to say no."

"Going to tell him the reason?"

"No," Charley answered hurriedly. "He has enough troubles of his own without burdening him with mine. I'll tell him something came up I have to deal with in Seattle next week, and I can't do that and be with him."

"Well, it has the benefit of being the truth. Just not the whole truth. Guess you really don't owe him that, do you?"

Charley studied her half-empty snifter glass. "Just met him. Barely know him."

Marla Jo knew her friend was physically and emotionally drained and didn't want to add to her awful plight by keeping her talking. She put her crystal glass by the sink and topped off Charley's brandy before hugging her and heading off to bed.

Charley lay awake for more than an hour. Frustrated, she threw on the terry cloth robe laid across the freshly made bed in the second-floor guest room and quietly slipped into the hallway. The Taylors had urged her to consider their home hers, so she felt comfortable making a cup of tea in their kitchen. While waiting for the water to boil, she washed both glasses and put them back in the cabinet she'd watched Marla Jo take them from.

Well past midnight, Charley settled into a chaise lounge inside the screened-in sun porch whose windows were closed tightly against the night air's chill. She recalled Marla Jo telling her that once the muggy June air was filled with the aroma of gardenias, she and Ben would crank open the windows and turn on the ceiling fan in anticipation of joyful evening serenades by a chorus of frogs, crickets, and possibly, cicadas.

A three-quarter incandescent moon against a partly cloudy early April sky illuminated the spreading crape myrtle trees methodically planted several feet apart many years ago to create a neighborly barrier on three sides of the Taylor residence.

Charley stretched her legs and crossed one ankle over the other as she held the cup and saucer with both hands. *How different this world is to the one waiting for me back in Seattle,* she thought.

Feeling adrift, an image of her late father slipped into her mind's eye, and her thoughts turned to how she'd arrived at this moment in time.

The Reverend Marshall Franklin Tuell had prayed his firstborn would be a son, someone to carry the family name and his profession into the next generation. A difficult birth meant there would be only one child, and Ruth Tuell resisted her husband's insistence on a biblical name. They baptized her Charlene Ann, and the third-generation Seattle minister nicknamed her Charley before she could walk. Early childhood teachers resisted, but Charley insisted, as only a headstrong child can. The nickname stuck in and out of the classroom. As she grew older, few came to know her given name, and that was fine by her.

Charley grew up in a loving Christian home that shaped her childhood thinking. She felt her heart and mind tugged toward what her father had wanted in a son. The feeling began while she attended a summer church retreat in Bend, Oregon, when she was not yet old enough to drive, and in the absence of any parental encouragement, only grew stronger with each passing year.

Reverand Tuell was adamant the ministry was not a woman's profession. Unless his daughter planned to be a professor or social worker, a seminary would waste her time and her parents' limited money. His wife remained ambivalent before ultimately siding with her daughter. Peace and harmony never fully returned to the Tuell household.

One thing that did unite Charley's father and mother while contributing to family inquietude was their disapproval of her marriage. Charley assured them it was love, not rebellion, underlying her desire to marry Richard Kersting right out of the liberal-leaning seminary where they'd met. She insisted she knew almost as much about her future husband as she did about herself and was beyond disappointed when her father refused to officiate her wedding. Richard's in-laws never relented in their distaste for him, taking their feelings to their graves within a few years of each other before Charley reached her mid-thirties.

Richard's first job as a youth minister in a small Tacoma church was a calling he felt hugely beneath him. His blend of movie star looks, natural charisma, and effortless eloquence fueled his thinly disguised aspiration to be the next Billy Graham. He turned his insatiable appetite for acclaim to publishing a bestselling Christian book. He convinced himself it would then be no great leap to all-important television exposure, and he'd be on his way.

Neither his lack of creative writing skills nor an original idea for compelling content dissuaded his thinking because he had a solution for both. Richard persuaded his young bride to write a book based on her seminary thesis about contentment.

Sitting on Marla Jo's porch, Charley remembered how she'd readily agreed to her then-husband's request for sole credit after he persuaded her that neither of them would want what would happen if she didn't. She recalled how she didn't think her first rough manuscript draft held much promise. As it turned out, she was as wrong about the book as she would come to be about so many other things in her husband's life.

Soon after the book hit the bestseller lists, Richard accepted the associate pastor role at a mega-church on Seattle's metropolitan eastside. Within a few years, he ascended to lead pastor because of the unfortunate hand dealt his predecessor, who succumbed to early-onset Parkinson's disease. Charley had wept for that pastor and his family, but Richard didn't believe it was at all unfortunate. Instead, it was one more step toward fulfilling the vision of his destiny.

Richard never publicly acknowledged Charley's contributions at any time in any way. He felt no gratitude to his wife for all the good things that happened to him and for him. He was in an unbridled hurry to reach his lofty goals. To the astonishment of almost everyone and the envy of many, he quickly assembled a half-dozen satellite churches across the Puget Sound area and negotiated a lucrative national television ministry. The wind was truly beneath his wings, and the money from devoted followers came pouring in. But in his mind, he was flying solo.

Looking out into the semi-darkness of the Taylor's backyard, Charley remembered feeling that she had no choice but to accept Richard's growing acclaim and constant travel. She loved her husband and wanted to be supportive. Since he didn't want her working outside their home or inside the church, she'd settled for being a pastor's dutiful stay-at-home wife raising their daughter. Like her father, her husband insisted on a biblical name. Unlike her mother, Charley had given in, and they named their only child Rachel.

For many years, the Kerstings fell into rituals carved out by their distinctly different public and private selves. Charley allowed herself to be bent to Richard's will, relegated to an appendage who put on a smiling face when trotted out for appearance's sake when it served her husband's interests. That happened almost always on Sunday.

She was never with him when he traveled, and as he soared to ever-increasing heights, Richard's investment in their marriage and parenting fell to almost nothing. Also lacking was his interest in their romantic life. Charley naturally became suspicious. The warning signs were there. In the early years, she endured the indignities as a form of penance for things she must have done wrong. Later, she simply accepted them as the price one pays to weather the "'till death do us part" alter pledge.

Charley took her last sip of tea and faintly smiled when recalling a time she and her best friend were young mothers together. After a bit too much wine at lunch, the other woman, slurring her words, offered her assessment that people, especially women, were drawn to Richard as the comic strip Pooh was drawn to his honey pot.

Charley wasn't blissfully unaware, but she didn't go searching, fearful of what she might find. Her worst fears at the time paled in comparison to what others eventually found when pulling back the curtain on the secret life of Richard Kersting. Only much later would she learn her "friend" had spoken that day from personal experience.

Her walk down memory lane had settled into the porch area like an unpleasant odor. She shook her head dolefully, then rose to re-enter the house. She placed the cup and saucer in the dishwasher and once again climbed the stairs. She couldn't stop recalling how much her actions, and inactions, had cost her, including the loss of her daughter's love.

And that phone call with her attorney kept playing over and over in her mind.

Charley first sought the high-profile lawyer when she'd learned Richard had signed an untruthful affidavit in which he described her as fully knowledgeable of his ministry's finances. She sat as motionless as a sleeping cat while the attorney speculated Richard's motive might be grounded in a narcissistic and mistaken belief that making her equally culpable would somehow alter the government's pursuit of him. Or at least burnish his image sufficiently to decrease his punishment. Charley heard the lawyer say Richard was most likely counting on the halo effect of her public persona—albeit tarnished—to do for him something that he would never do for her if the roles were reversed.

But all of that had occurred months before her lawyer's call interrupted her dinner with David, and she learned her ex-husband had been found dead in a hotel room three hours north of Seattle, just across the Canadian border in Vancouver. The lawyer said no foul play was suspected, but did know how her ex-husband's affidavit would now darkly color Charley's future. Because Richard had fled the country, Charley heard bail for her was far from assured, even after she surrendered her passport.

Lying wide awake in someone else's bed in the middle of the night in Kentucky, Charley knew her public shame would only worsen upon her return. The growing estrangement from her daughter left her with the same monumental feeling of emptiness she'd known only too well in her marriage. Playing the same old movies in her head, she entered the familiar darkness of depression and the attendant thoughts of suicide. Her only consolation came with the knowledge that at least her parents weren't alive to witness the unfolding of her prime-time drama.

Richard had never allowed Charley any knowledge of their finances; thus she was stunned by the high six-figure divorce settlement she received. With no clear thoughts about her future, she'd moved to a small furnished apartment on Bainbridge, one of the San Juan Islands reached by ferry from Seattle. That's where she was living when contacted by a literary agent with the idea of a book of her own, a suggestion that led to the Bowling Green trip and into the life of one David Jacobs . . . and his dreams.

Thinking of David brought a smile to her face and a welcome sense of peacefulness. Because of him, her world—at least for now and no telling how long—had become a better place. She made her decision. It was her last thought before she fell asleep.

In a hotel near the town square, the uncertainty of Charley's answer the next day left David's world in limbo and sleep elusive. Sprawled across the bed, he tossed and turned for half an hour before giving up. He pulled on jeans and a wrinkled shirt, tucked his Corvette owner's manual under one arm, and walked down three flights of stairs to the comfortable lobby. His appearance was about as disheveled as he would ever permit in public, but he was fairly certain he would be the only public at this hour of the morning. Sitting in a comfortable chair with his feet resting on a matching ottoman, he hoped the detailed handbook would prepare him to master the intricacies of his new car and bring on much-needed sleep.

His passion for owning a Corvette enabled him to devour the book's often excruciating detail. Still, he found his concentration occasionally broken by reflective thoughts about the seasons of his life. He moved to America from Australia, staying on when his reason for coming no longer existed, reaching mid-life without a wife or children, and mired in his memories yet crippled by awareness of the ever-quickening downward flow of sand in his hourglass of life. Things he'd kept from the alluring woman he feared would not join him later in the day.

After several hours, David was unable to keep his eyes open. He closed the thick leather binder and returned to his room. The LED clock on the bedside table gleamed *2:58* in red numerals. He set an alarm on the clock and his phone to roust him for his appointment in a few hours. His last waking thoughts were of Charley Chaplain.

～

David's red carpet "pre-flight" consultation was conducted in the expansive lobby of the Corvette Museum by an attractive automotive engineer in her early thirties wearing khaki slacks and a starched, long-sleeved white shirt with a Corvette logo sewn on the left pocket.

The process went by relatively quickly because of his hours of early morning study.

After less than an hour of orientation, he looked at his watch and assumed the worst about Route 66 and the woman he'd hoped would accompany him on his dream journey.

The engineer, standing only a few steps away from David and his now-realized four-wheel dream, told him in an accent that marked her as a local, "Mr. Jacobs, something to keep in mind. Try to become as familiar with your new car's workings as you are with everything you have in your wallet."

"Clever. And Darla, I bet you tell every new owner that."

The petite woman shyly looked away for a moment before her violet eyes connected with his, and she smiled broadly.

"Not true. I save it only for new owners who meet special criteria."

"That being?"

She'd demonstrated supreme confidence when talking at length about David's car, but she now took on an air of demureness. "Handsome Australian men not in the company of a female companion."

"I see. Well, I'm both appreciative . . . and curious."

"Curious about what?"

"Is this special criteria you speak of one created by General Motors?"

If possible, she smiled even more broadly when she shook her head.

"May I ask how many have gone before me?" he asked.

"Well, Mr. Jacobs, I'm not the least bit embarrassed to tell you . . . you're the first."

"And you shouldn't be. You've done a marvelous job getting me oriented, and for that I'm very grateful. Especially for coming in on a Saturday morning."

"It's my job." She used two hands to slowly place both sets of keys into just one of his hands. "And if you want, we can take a longer test drive after I get off work."

Striving to sound both innocent and uncertain, he asked, "Darla, are you flirting with me?"

"Yes, sir, Mr. Jacobs, I guess I am."

"It's my accent, isn't it? Go on, you can tell me the truth."

"Yeah." Then she hurriedly added, "But, well, I guess . . ."

It took only a second for an image of Charley to enter his mind. "I'm flattered. I truly am. But I'm spoken for."

Before she could reply, he confounded her by asking if she was the person to help with arrangements to ship his new Corvette to California.

Darla started to speak when David's phone vibrated in his pocket.

# 7

## *Dream Coming True*

"**Y**ou lied to me."

Matter-of-fact intonation in Charley's voice diluted any harshness in her accusatory words. At least, that's what David told himself as he inhaled the intoxicating new car smell.

Eyes fixed on the road ahead, hands firmly on the leather-wrapped, squared-off steering wheel, he politely asked, "How's that again?"

"You *know* what I mean. You said this was a car like any other. Those were your exact words. And my little bit of online research yesterday didn't prepare me. I mean, this is more like a European race car. Or at least what I'd imagine one to be. No wonder there's so little trunk space."

"Boot."

"Boot? Boot what?"

"Europeans mostly refer to the luggage compartment as a boot. Australians, too."

The confining interior of the small, two-door car didn't hinder the stringing-up of a now-familiar verbal volleyball net.

"I see. Tell me, will it be like this all the way to California? The gracious passenger and the smartass Aussie driver?"

He cocked his head from side to side and, with a smartass grin, replied, "I guess time will tell."

"Oh, joy."

Less than two hours earlier, David had resigned himself to a flight home, his dream unrealized. Thrilled wouldn't begin to describe how he'd felt when Charley called saying she'd go with him . . . if he still wanted her to.

He tried to resist a first-thought impulse . . . but couldn't.

"I don't know, Charley. You seemed so uncertain last night. And, well, I've discovered this morning that a new Corvette gets a lot of attention from admiring women."

Banter-up.

"You paid a hundred grand to attract women in a town where you don't live and may never return? Seems like a solid investment to me. And I'm sure you can persuade one of them to drop every-thing and go with you. I'll tell Marla Jo I changed my mind and go shopping with her in Nashville today. It was nice meeting you. Travel safely."

"No, no," he answered hurriedly, pressing his cell phone tighter to his ear. "Only kidding."

She felt turnabout would be fair play and waited out the Mississippi count he'd used so effectively with her the night they met. *Could that have been only a day and a half ago?*

"So am I, Mr. Hollywood Screenwriter," she finally assured him. "So am I."

David knew the way to the Taylor residence but still engaged the sophisticated GPS. While he showed an enthusiastic and envious Ben the finer points of the Corvette Stingray gleaming in the morning sunlight, Charley took one quick look at the interior and turned heel back toward the front door, saying she needed time to repack.

"Yeah, I know, space is limited," David called after her. "Just throw a few things together. We don't need to impress each other. At least, I don't need impressing. And we can buy anything we need along the way.

"Easy for you to say," she replied, frustration evident in each word.

"Hey, I'm sacrificing, too."

Standing with one leg inside the doorway, Charley asked, "In what way?"

"I dunno. I'm sure I am. I'll think of it before you get back."

While Charley rummaged through the clothes she'd packed before leaving Seattle, she didn't second-guess her impulsive, middle-of-the-night decision. The thrill of an uncertain, cross-country adventure with a man she'd so quickly become attracted to had replaced some of the feelings of self-pity over what awaited her in Seattle. If she chose to return.

Although the Corvette had respectable front and rear storage space for a car its size, Ben and Marla Jo readily agreed to ship home Charley's two large suitcases with most of what she'd brought with her. They extended the same courtesy to David. Hugs, handshakes, and goodbyes behind them, the two travelers headed north.

Almost as soon as David pulled onto Interstate 65, he pointed out the Corvette plant and the National Corvette Museum, both easily visible off to the left.

"How busy was the maternity ward yesterday?"

"Very," he replied. "I learned every Corvette since 1981 has been born there."

"Tell me about this one. And please, not like you would tell Ben. Pretend you're talking to an unenthusiastic sixth-grader."

"Happy to." *Where to begin?* "You may not have noticed, but the hard top is retractable. It can become an open-air convertible. Accounts for some of the limited boot space."

"You're right. Missed that."

"Okay. Quickly. Keyless remote engine start-up and entry. Gear changes, as you can see here, are push buttons. If you were sitting where I'm sitting, some instrumentation, like the speedometer, is displayed on the windshield in front of the driver." He pointed to the tablet-like display jutting out from the dashboard between them. "On this screen are all kinds of things I can call up with finger touches, just like an iPad."

"For example?"

"Well, there are different modes for features like firmness for brakes and steering."

"I'm sure there are. Do these *features* have names?" she asked, certain they did.

"Regular, what we're experiencing now. Sport and track."

"Let's stick with regular for now. And David, trust me when I say I'm *never* trading places with you."

"Understood." A few seconds ticked by. "Two consequences, though."

"What?"

"Our trip will take a few days longer."

"You told me that last night."

"And Sheila will be disappointed not to experience a woman's touch."

"You named your car Sheila?"

He gave a sideward nod, eyes ahead.

She decided it would be a long trip indeed if she began responding to his head movements and hand gestures. It took a bit of time before her silent message sank in.

"I did," he replied.

"I know you're just dying for me to ask why."

"Got it from my mother. She always named her cars. At least for the time she was with us."

Charley distinctly heard his last sentence and filed it away to revisit another time.

"Okay. I'll indulge you. How'd you pick Sheila? Memorable lady in your past or present? An actress, perhaps?'

"You asked if you'd be hearing more Aussie slang. Sheila is a fairly common term for a woman among men in Oz. Especially if she's attractive." He thought that would elicit a response. It didn't. "My good fortune today is traveling with one while driving one."

"Can't speak for the other Sheila, but your flattery has certainly turned my head. Permission granted to keep it up. Sincerity required." She paused. "Is there a similar name for Australian men?"

"Yeah. Bruce."

"Seriously?"

"Seriously."

"Well, I have nothing to offer on that. But I do have a question. A moment ago, you said Oz. As in the Wizard of?"

"Not at all. More slang. A common abbreviation of Australia is the first three letters. There can be a bit of a hissing sound when spoken, so it comes out Oz."

Charley's mind went in another direction, to the limited number of personal belongings she could bring along. Scaled back makeup and toiletries, two pairs of designer jeans (she was wearing one), a handful of blouses, one sweater, and a couple of pairs of shoes. She'd definitely hold him to his promise to purchase items along the way since her idea of "roughing it" was when her hotel room faced a wooded area, and room service ended before the ten o'clock news.

"Back to the other Sheila," she said. "I'm curious about your color selections. Not being critical, mind you. Just not what I would've thought went with a woman's name."

David had selected Ceramic Matrix Gray Metallic from among fourteen possibilities and Adrenaline Red for the plush, hand-stitched leather interior.

"Certainly not the most popular combinations, I'll grant you that. But the two colors appealed to me in a car I saw on a showroom floor in California. Before that, when I first started getting serious about buying one, my thinking was combinations of red, white, and blue."

"You *actually* considered spending a small fortune to get a car that reminds you of the flag? You're that Americanized?"

David smiled.

This time, she didn't wait for him to speak.

"What?" she asked.

"Ever seen the Australian flag?

"What was it you said so eloquently a little while ago? Oh, yes. I dunno." She paused. "Let me guess. Same colors?"

"More like blue, red, and white than red, white, and blue."

"Stumbled into that one. And boy, do I feel stupid. But very American, I guess."

"Oh, don't be so hard on yourself." He changed the subject. "Comfortable?"

She moved her shoulders back and forth. "Taking some getting used to. Feels like a small airplane. Been in those before. Really tight."

"That it is. As was the Concorde, I understand, back in its day.

Speed necessitates compromise, I suppose. I guess it's a good thing neither of us is claustrophobic."

Not a good guess. Charley *was* claustrophobic. And for circumstances when she wasn't in control, like being a passenger in a car or an airplane, she had prescription medicine as a temporary antidote. She'd taken a pill at Marla Jo's house when she got her first good look inside Sheila and doubted that King County back in Washington would accommodate her special need if she found herself confined to a six-by-nine-foot jail cell—a thought that haunted her.

Many words could describe the passing terrain of rolling hills and farms interspersed with truck stop exits, but in David's mind, "memorable" wouldn't be one of them. Though not unlike nondescript billboard-laden interstate highways crossing the country, the area presented a palate of nothingness compared to what he anticipated ahead on Route 66.

An hour later, traffic became heavier as they approached the outskirts of Louisville. David moved away from making small talk and asked Charley a question she'd been expecting.

"May I ask what troubled you so much about your phone call last night? Asking only as a way of offering to help, if possible. Or wanted."

"Oh, nothing much," she answered, slowly parsing her words, trying for nonchalance. "And nothing you can help with." She nervously swallowed. "Just that my ex-husband had been found dead in a hotel room in Canada. That's all."

David thought about leaving well enough alone but couldn't muster sufficient restraint.

"You were a chaplain. Now, you're not. You were married, now you're not. Your former husband might have still been alive when we met, but now you've learned he's not. How does one go from where you were to where you are now?"

Charley sat in silence.

71

"Wanna talk about it?"

"No, I don't," she answered emphatically. "Not now. It's a very long story, the one you're so anxious to hear. He was a big part of it. I'm certain your persistence will coax it out of me before we get to California."

The only sound was road noise, though minimal due to Corvette's leading-edge engineering.

After a while, David wanted to know more and shifted the conversation away from Charley's husband but kept it in her family. "Marla Jo told me you had a daughter. Living in California, I think."

"Rachel."

"With what happened to her father, don't you need to get back to be with her?"

Although well-intended, David's question caused Charley to think the bottom had truly dropped out of her life.

"I had to choose." She paused, then softly said, "I chose you."

David's grip on the wheel tightened to keep Sheila from swerving across the center line. Recovering, he said, "And I'll be indebted to you forever. But are you sure you made the right decision? We can turn back."

*A dead, despicable husband. An estranged daughter. A blood-thirsty media. Certainty of incarceration. Who would have chosen Seattle over this—whatever "this" turns out to be?*

With a look of profound sorrow, she replied, "It wasn't as difficult a decision as you might think."

Charley and her husband had been living separate lives while sharing the same residence. He'd messed with her mind in so many ways for so long that she had no inkling of the cascading assertions leveled against him about things far worse than what she'd suspected. First, one woman came forward with allegations, and then a stream of others followed. When the local media began mining the drama to fill its pages and newscasts, intrepid reporters also began sniffing out rumors of financial shenanigans within the vast Kersting ministry, and some were rewarded with bold headlines for their efforts. Ripping a page out of the playbook of fallen television evangelists who had gone before him, Richard took to the pulpit more than once to tearfully plead a lie-filled concoction of innocence to his Seattle congregations and his national audience.

Charley looked at David's profile and longed for a sorcerer who could turn the calendar back so they could have met at a different time under different circumstances. She looked to her right, taking in the passing skyline of Kentucky's largest city. "Can we not talk for a while?"

They drove across the towering four-lane bridge that spanned the Ohio River, carrying them into Indiana. The muted road sounds became white noise that lulled Charley to sleep; she didn't wake until an hour had passed. Rubbing her eyes and still a bit groggy, she turned toward David.

"I want to be a good traveling companion. I really do. But can we talk about something besides ourselves for at least one day?"

"Absolutely. Anything come to mind?"

"Yes. This road that has you so enchanted."

"I'm all in for that. Can you get an internet browser on your cell phone?"

"I can. Or at least I could in Seattle."

"Why don't you give it a try and search for Route 66."

It took a couple of minutes before Charley began reading out loud.

"Known at various times by various names. America's Highway. Main Street of America. Main Street USA. The Mother Road. The Will Rogers Highway. It goes on to say Route 66 is a fabled ribbon of asphalt and concrete that winds across eight states covering well over two thousand miles."

"More like twenty-four hundred, I think. Please help me remember the states . . . east to west."

"Let's see. Give me a minute. Okay. Starting in Chicago, it would be Illinois. Then Missouri, Kansas, Oklahoma, Texas, and New Mexico. The last two are Arizona and California."

"Thanks. I think I had them all in mind except for Kansas."

"And this is interesting. At least, I think it is. Because people steal the signs for souvenirs, in some places the symbol and the number have been painted right onto the highway itself."

"Sad. But then again, I'm not surprised," David replied. "Things being what they are these days."

"Says here there was a television show for a few years back in the sixties named *Route 66*."

"I've watched all the episodes on streaming channels over the past few years. I also know any number of articles and books have been written about it. I seem to recall John Steinbeck calling it the mother road in his book *The Grapes of Wrath*."

"Even more interesting. Say, David, I'm reading that not all of the original road is drivable, and some of it no longer exists. Do you know how much is still left?"

"My friend Mac thinks quite a bit of it, winding its way back and forth near interstate highways. But that's just a guess. We'll certainly find out. Part of what makes this an adventure."

"Are you sure you want to drive this beautiful new car over roads like that?"

"You bet. As I've said, Sheila's just a car—"

"I know. Like any other."

The hour-and-a-half drive from the Ohio River to the light Sunday afternoon traffic on the I-465 Beltway encircling Indianapolis was uneventful—and far from scenic.

"Charley, you might be interested to know there are more interstate highways connecting the city of Indianapolis than anywhere else in the country."

"Good to know. And you're quite the repository of random facts, aren't you?"

"A bit of a left-handed compliment," he answered with a crooked smile, "but yes, I guess I am."

"Are you by chance studying to be on Jeopardy?"

"Clever. And, I might add, quick."

"Learning from the master. Or trying to."

Gaining confidence by the hour behind the wheel of Sheila, David deftly steered in and out of traffic. The flatland vistas of chiefly farmland remained unremarkable as they trekked onward until they passed the exits to Lafayette, home of Purdue University, and encountered mile after mile of hundreds of towering gray windmills connected to turbines in nearby solar farms on both sides of the highway.

"They look like giant prehistoric birds," Charley observed. "Without heads."

"That they do."

In the summer, this part of Indiana was prone to tornadoes, and in the winter, windswept snow often shut down roads and highways. But on this day, sun-drenched blue skies and mild temperatures. At Merrillville, David made a sweeping left turn to enter the main artery of eight-lane Chicago traffic that began thirty miles or so away from the city limits. Weekends offered little relief from congestion—and the abundance of reckless drivers.

Charley knew David had to be nervous and didn't distract him with idle conversation.

David didn't relax until he'd guided his new car under the porte-cochere at the five-star downtown hotel holding their reservations, a place he'd selected for its indoor valet parking to house both Sheilas safely for the night.

They each carried an overnight bag to the marble check-in counter, where David presented a credit card, and they separately filled out registration forms. Two rooms had been reserved; the different floors were the luck of the draw that unnecessarily reinforced the assurances David had given Charley.

As they stood in front of the shiny brass framework of the lobby elevators, Charley apologized for cutting short a conversation about her ex-husband's death.

"Unfair to dump that on you and then just leave it."

"Didn't bother me in the least. Do you want to talk about it?"

"No, but I feel I have to. Get it behind us before your magical journey begins."

"*Our* magical journey."

*Would that it could be,* she thought.

The elevator door opened, they stepped in, and David pushed two buttons. As the door closed, Charley said, "Here's a thought. Since we don't really know each other . . . well, that's not true, is it? You know a lot about me, and I know virtually nothing about you. True?"

David continued to withhold what he'd learned from Marla Jo and disagreed.

"Whatever. Anyway, despite what I asked for earlier, I was thinking that over dinner . . . we are having dinner, aren't we?"

David nodded

"Over dinner tonight, we tell each other our stories and get that behind us before we set out on *our* magical journey in the morning."

"Wonderful idea. We'll just kick back and plumb the depths of old memories. And miseries." The door opened to Charley's floor. As she stepped out, he added. "Ladies first."

"No," she answered as she turned back toward him. "Tonight it's ladies' *choice*. You share first." As the door closed, she added,

"And remember, since Marla Jo isn't here, you still don't have to use big words."

Later on, taking separate elevators minutes apart to meet again for story time, they both had the same thought: *When you have no future, you live in the past.*

# 8

## Story Time

"Not much to tell, really," David said. "And certainly no der-ring-do if that's what you're hoping for."

Determined not to lose patience even before Sheila's tires had touched Route 66, Charley remained silent. They were waiting for their modest dinners in the hotel's showy yet cozy coffee shop, and when he didn't continue, her fingernails clicked impatiently on the white laminate tabletop.

"Okay," he said in surrender. "You win. For now."

She winked above the lip of her cup of decaffeinated coffee. "And you have my undivided attention."

"The night we met, I told you I was born and raised in Adelaide. Attended university in Sydney, and stayed on there to work. When I said I was somewhat Americanized, I was minimizing."

*Imagine that*, Charley thought.

"My father was an American diplomat assigned to the consulate office, and through his work, met my mother, an Australian econo-mist. They married, and a year or so later, along I came." He drank some iced tea. "Both were Jewish, though neither was terribly serious about it. Their faith, that is, not their heritage."

"Are they still alive? I ask because my parents aren't."

David watched Charley use her fork to surgically remove every piece of ham from her chef salad and carefully place each one on an unused bread plate.

"No. They're both gone. Quite some time ago. After they passed, I became close to my mother's two brothers, Sid and Victor. Great guys and very successful in the car business. They treated me more like one of their sons than a nephew."

"Brothers or sisters?" she asked as she folded in blue cheese dressing.

"Only child. Although my mother had two brothers and a sister, she was fond of saying 'one and done.' He never said it outright, but my father often gave the impression he wanted more. Or at least that's the way I remember it."

"And you. Ever married? Children, either here or there?"

"No, and no."

Between bites of his Reuben sandwich, David told Charley that after a stint as a writer with *The Sydney Morning Herald*, he followed a woman to America. She was an aspiring actress, so they settled in New York City, where he worked as a freelance writer.

"After a couple of years, she left me. I stayed on in the city and became a foreign correspondent for the *Herald*, mostly writing about life as an expat in America."

He told her he'd found the newspaper business didn't provide the challenge he wanted and discovered he had a knack for writing off-Broadway plays. After making ends meet for a few years, he took to heart the advice of others and headed off to Hollywood to try his hand at becoming a screenwriter.

"I made my way to the Left Coast, and things sorta worked out nicely. I was earning a respectable living, so I put down roots."

"Would I recognize anything you worked on?"

Charley was impressed, as anyone would be, hearing just a few of the movies and television shows he'd written for, either in whole or in part. If there was an "in part," he told her it often involved his friend Mac. Anticipating she might ask, David mentioned he had three novels in various stages of completion, stopping well short of confessing they never would be.

David Jacobs was a man in his fifty-sixth year who had little hope of living beyond his coming October birthday. He was truthful when he told Charley he lived in California. What he didn't tell her was that while he still owned a home there, he'd established residency in Oregon to hopefully qualify for legally assisted suicide when the time came.

Grateful for a serious conversation free of quips and teasing, Charley said, "Thank you for sharing. I'm sure there's a lot more, and we still have several days ahead of us."

"I assure you, unlike yours, my life story is a shallow pond. And we've just waded in knee-deep, touching bottom."

"What a turn of phrase." She shook her head. "But I ain't buyin' it."

He chewed the last of his sandwich thoughtfully and set his plate aside. "Be that as it may, your turn."

With her salad only partially eaten, she laid her fork down and asked what Marla Jo had told him. Once again, he disclosed little of what he had learned from their mutual friend and his recent online reading about Seattle's Charley Chaplain.

"David, I know we're both tired. Or at least I am. I'll be as brief as you were."

"As long as you don't leave out any juicy parts."

*He certainly is easy to talk with. More so than any man I've ever known.*

"I'll leave it to you to be the arbiter of what qualifies in your mind as juicy."

Like re-reading a book she'd just finished, Charley covered select portions of what had kept her awake into the early morning hours. Her words were devoid of emotion, and David listened without interrupting. She wasn't going anywhere without him for a least a week— or so he thought. She concluded her story before reaching the fate awaiting her return to Seattle.

"I know I've talked a lot about Richard, but he defined me for a long time. Over twenty-five years. He just seemed... larger than life. Certainly larger than *my* life while we were together, and other people saw him that way too. They worshipped him." She looked away, then back. "I'm curious what Marla Jo told you about him."

"Nothing much, really. Just his name and a description."

"Interesting. How'd she describe someone she's never met?"

"Eloquently, though succinctly. Only three words, as I recall."

Her eyes grew wider in anticipation.

"And they were . . .?"

"Piece of shit."

"That *is* rather succinct. Don't know about the eloquent part."

"From what you've just shared, doesn't appear she was wrong."

"Sadly, she wasn't. And neither were my parents."

*No surprise there*, he thought. "They didn't like him?"

"After being around Richard for only a little while before we got married, Daddy sat me down in his church office and told me 'something's not right about this guy.' He went on to say—and I remember his exact words to this day—'he may seem all polished on the outside, but I know there's rust underneath. And you won't have to scratch too hard to find it.'"

"Good fatherly instincts."

"Wish I'd listened to him." She seemed to drift away for a moment. "I could be a little stubborn back then."

"Have you gotten over it?"

"The stubbornness?"

He nodded.

"You tell me . . . when we finally get to where we're going."

"Fair enough. Charley, you mentioned your ex's book. Confess I haven't read it and—"

"Because it's not in Hebrew?"

"Cute. But I understand a lot of others have."

"A *lot* of others," she echoed, with an edge to her voice.

"One thing Marla Jo did tell me was that your ex didn't write the book. You did."

This time, it was Charley who nodded.

"Were you surprised by what happened?"

"Totally."

"I understand it was a bestseller. Did he acknowledge you in any way?"

"No. Never. But I don't mind. Didn't then, and don't now."

"Why? I'd think most people in similar circumstances would. Me included."

"Perhaps. But at the same time, neither of us wanted a Jim and Tammy Fay comparison, one Richard so vividly described as inevitable if he shared his glory with me. The truth is, I'd written something I didn't think anyone would be interested in, especially if they had to pay for it."

"Yet, at the end of the day, you made him a rock star."

"Actually, I helped create a monster. One with a callous heart, at least toward me and our daughter."

"Was he unfaithful to you?"

Her bitter smile gave a silent answer. "He didn't even have to go looking. Women were drawn to him. Either misguided or simply out for a celebrity conquest."

"But you were suspicious, right?"

"It's amazing what you can ignore when you put your mind to it."

"Looking at all this a bit differently," David said, "did *you* make your husband jealous by being with uniformed men at all hours?"

"To the moon and back. I lived with a constant drumbeat of accusations, and it took a long time to realize it was all meant to keep *me* off-balance so I wouldn't suspect *his* playing around."

"With him being a Christian media darling, the story got quite a lot of attention in California for a time. What I remembered most—before meeting you—was his colossal fall from grace."

Sitting in that hotel café, Charley became an island unto herself for several moments.

"And he took me down with him," she finally said.

David paused and absently played with a spoon before asking, "What about your daughter?"

"That's the real tragedy in all of this."

"In what way?"

Charley told him her daughter had begged her many times to divorce, saying over and over they both knew he was guilty as sin. As many sins.

"So when you chose instead to stand by him—"

"We haven't spoken since. Just a few texts."

"If leaving him wouldn't turn your daughter against you, and it sounds like it wouldn't, why didn't you heed her pleadings?"

Although confident Richard was lying about everything, Charley had come to the uncomfortable conclusion that the divorce her daughter urged would eventually destroy his ministry and bring despair to many of the hundreds of thousands of lives he touched every week. And possibly bring ruin to some of the families whose livelihoods depended upon him. She knew he skated near the edge without knowing where the cliff ended and the falloff began. He lived as though he were playing tennis with the net down. Conflicted and wanting more time to decide, she reluctantly gave one appearance, and only one, of standing by her man worthy of the country music song. Over time, as Richard's house of cards collapsed, being shunned by friends and professional colleagues became an unintended consequence of Charley's decision.

Her eyes grew moist, and she dabbed at her tears with her napkin.

"Want me to shut up about all this?" David asked.

Charley shook her head.

"Should have listened to Rachel and others." She let out a long breath. "I have so many regrets . . . this being the most profound."

David looked away to signal their waitress, and Charley stifled a yawn.

"Charley, I know it's been a very long day for both of us, but I have just one more question."

"Okay."

"There must have been a tipping point that caused you to finally turn away from him."

His curiosity forced her to smile for the first time.

"Well, here's a not-so-original story idea for one of your screenplays. I found out one of Richard's playmates for several years was the person I thought was my best friend. We lived in the same neighborhood and raised our children together. Someone in whom I felt I could confide anything, including some of my most personal thoughts about my husband. I'm sure it all made for wonderful pillow talk between them." Beneath the table, she closed her hand into a fist. "I was devastated."

He paused long enough to consider the wisdom of sharing his thoughts. He recalled reading somewhere a marriage tops any list of complicated relationships.

"I can relate."

"How?" she asked with a disbelieving tone. "You said you were never married."

"True. Left out something from my story. Something I guess most folks would deem juicy."

David's mother had been distant and moody, but he'd been close to his father, especially in his teen years. While he was away at university, his mother took a lover the same age as her son, and the two of them left for a life together in Perth on the opposite side of the vast country. His father, having willingly displaced himself from his own country rather than ask his Australian wife to leave hers, became a humiliated and broken man. David never forgave his mother, and seethed with anger each time he recalled the man who had replaced his father in his mother's bed was David's best friend from childhood. His father fell on hard times, became a heavy drinker, and died in a one-car accident a year later.

David told Charley he never saw his mother again and was on holiday in Tasmania when she passed away. He learned of her death from one of her brothers after her funeral, a service he said he would not have attended even if he had known.

"It brought me close to my uncles. A few years later, I left for America."

"Well, it seems I certainly don't have a lock on sad stories, do I?"

David crossed his arms over his chest. "No one does. Life isn't always fair. Never has been, never will be. I think most everyone has their own boulevard of broken dreams."

"Beautifully said. Though no surprise. David, may I balance the scale by asking one more question of you?"

"Of course."

"You said the woman you followed to New York left you. What happened?"

He thought about how infidelity had created a symbolic inter-section of their two lives long before they met a few days ago. He uncrossed his arms to pick up the check their waitress left on the edge of the table, added a generous tip when he charged their meals to his room, and turned the slip of paper face down.

"I guess in one way, you and I are kindred souls. Mine was not at all a unique refrain in the annals of the theater world. She dumped me for a producer with whom she was having an affair."

"Were you devastated when it happened?"

"Not really. We never quarreled, at least not that I recall, but I sensed it coming for quite some time. Nothing to cry the blues over. She thought he could help advance her career. We both moved on."

Charley was beginning to relish what she hoped was a growing friendship and silently wished the woman was in an obscure loca-tion, waitressing or bartending, struggling to pay her rent.

"I know about you. Or think I do. How'd that work out for her?"

"For the most part, I'd say rather well. Broadway, then Hollywood. Now both."

With a teasing smile, she asked, "Is her name a secret? Like your friend Mac and your pen name?"

He shook his head and told her.

Charley leaned back against her chair and almost keeled over.

"Seriously?"

"Seriously."

"Wow! She's . . . I mean she's really, you know—"

"Famous?" he asked.

"Understated, as you so often are, but yes!"

"Yeah, she's done okay . . . after not having me as an anchor to drag around."

"You don't believe that, and neither do I. Since you're both in the movie business, do you ever see her? Talk to her?"

"From time to time. And when she was cast in one of the movies I was involved with. But it's been a few years."

"So, you wrote the words, she spoke and acted them out. And became a movie star. Doesn't sound like much of an anchor."

David tapped his watch.

"End of story hour?" she asked.

They walked down the empty hallway toward the lobby. Until they reached the bank of elevators, the only sound they heard was their footsteps on stone flooring.

"David, we asked each other a lot of questions, but you left a big one out."

"What?"

"You never asked if I was faithful to Richard. Only if he was jealous."

"No need. I knew at least that much about you before you told me your story."

"And why were you . . . are you . . . so certain? You barely know me."

"Confucious."

"Confucious?"

"Yep. He said something about studying a person's words and behavior since both are paths to betrayal that can't be disguised."

The elevator doors opened.

"That's quite poignant, even for you. Is our evening going to end with Confucious?"

His smile momentarily lifted the travel fatigue from his voice and his face. "If you're half as tired as I am, it will have to."

# 9

# *The Journey Begins*

**D**avid's parting words had been to forget about setting alarms and sleep in. A noticeably refreshed Charley entered the lobby shortly after nine the next morning and found him sitting in an over-stuffed leather chair, drinking coffee, and studying a travel guide.

He stood as she approached. "You look lovely. Sleep well?"

"I did. And thank you." She spread her arms apart. "You said there'd be no need to impress you with a stunning wardrobe, so this is as good as it's gonna get."

*This* being snug-fitting black designer jeans and a cream-colored silk blouse that clung perfectly to her shoulders and draped over her waist, her appearance accentuated by pink and white running shoes.

"And you look mighty fine yourself." David wore matching black jeans and a muted-yellow golf shirt, polo style, with a small, multi-colored shark emblem near the left lapel—the brand of Australian golfer, Greg Norman. Brown leather slip-on driving shoes.

"I have a question," Charley said.

"Yes?"

"Not being critical. Oh, I think I said that about Sheila yesterday. Sorry. Anyway, just curious. Do you ever wear socks?"

"Only with my cowboy boots, the ones that didn't make the trip. Remember me telling you I also made sacrifices when you had to repack?"

"I do."

"Well, there you go."

David gestured to the matching chair next to his and eyed the self-service lobby bar. "Coffee?"

"That'd be wonderful."

"Cream. Right?"

She smiled, nodded, and watched him walk away. *Despite the Route 66 vagaries in the days ahead, this just feels right*, she thought. She knew she'd made the right decision and found herself almost giddy with excitement. When he returned, she asked where they would spend the night.

"St. Louis. Looks to be something less than three hundred miles. Even with our casual start, it's easily doable in a day. And my promise to you will always be the best places I can find with indoor parking . . . for both Sheilas."

"Starting early with the cute stuff, are we?"

David lifted his coffee cup. "A promise made, a promise kept," he replied, telling himself he was one lucky Bruce.

They each ate a toasted bagel from the lobby bar and agreed to forgo a larger breakfast, waiting instead for a satisfying lunch, ideally one with local flair, somewhere along the way. David generously tipped the parking valet, then maneuvered through bumper-to-bumper traffic to what for Route 66 travelers going west to east would be "trail's end"—the intersection of Adams Street and Michigan Avenue in downtown Chicago. For David and Charley, it marked the beginning.

By the time they reached the city limits, the morning skies had darkened, and thunderclouds moved in quickly. Less than fifty miles from their start, any sound from the windshield wipers was drowned out by the rain drumming a steady cadence on the roof as they passed through Joliet. Statesville prison, immortalized in *The Blues Brothers* movie, was a blur off the right side of the car.

Another eighty miles or so of David playing it safe with cautious driving brought them to Bloomington/Normal, often listed as one of the country's best college towns. The rain clouds eventually dissipated, and after traveling a hundred and forty miles, they stopped for lunch in McLean.

Seated opposite Charley in a corner booth, David looked around. "We gotta quit meeting like this. First Karen's Kastle, and now—"

"That's not very nice," she gently scolded.

"Yeah. But my promise to you was the best of everything. Concerned you might be disappointed."

"Now you're just being silly. I love simple, down-home places, and I bet you do, too."

"I do. And the two we've found thus far made special by the company I'm keeping."

"Fair warning. Keep up the flattery, and I'll grow accustomed to it."

After their orders were taken, Charley noticed two uniformed paramedics, a slightly overweight middle-aged man and a trim woman in her early twenties, sitting at a nearby table, preparing to leave. Charley gestured for their waitress and asked her to add the paramedics' meals to their check. When learning of her "pay it forward" kindness, the first responders stopped by to express their gratitude before they left.

A slight man in his seventies, dressed in faded bib overalls and a flannel shirt, pushed back the chair from his empty table. He removed his well-worn FDNY baseball cap as he slowly approached.

"Pardon me, ma'am," he said, his words unfalteringly polite, "I couldn't help noticing what you did. I also wanted to thank you."

Charley smiled. "Always a pleasure to do something for those who do so much."

David's eyes focused on the man's cap. "Were you there? On September 11th?"

The man scratched his stubbled cheek. "Yes, I was."

David extended his hand, and the man grasped it firmly.

"This is Charley. I'm David. And we want to thank you."

"Name's Lewis. Lewis Ernst. I'm called Lew."

David's professional life was all about creating imaginary characters, first in his mind, then on paper. He began to commit the man's walnut-textured face to memory—a wizened visage David thought could easily fold into recurring grief over that tragic September morning.

Lew smoothed his thinning white hair with one hand and tipped his hat with the other. "Now you good folks have a wonderful rest of your day." His scuffed boots shuffled a few steps back toward his table, where an open menu lay on top.

David understood Charley's inquiring look and nodded.

"Pardon me, Lew." The man turned toward Charley's voice. "If you're eating alone, we'd be honored if you'd join us."

"I'd like that. I'd like that very much." He looked at their small booth and suggested they might be more comfortable at his table.

Once they were all settled, David and Charley on one side, the man on the other, David asked, "Are you a local, Mr. Lewis?"

"Lew."

Charley tightened her lips and turned them inward to hold back a smile.

"Right," David acknowledged.

"And yessir, I am. Not forever, just a long time."

"Then may we prevail upon you for lunch recommendations?" David asked.

Charley was struck by how that formal phrasing seemed to convey that David was intimidated and rested her hand on his. "We've already ordered."

Charley and Lew exchanged smiles.

Regaining his composure, David asked, "So Lew, you were a firefighter in New York City. I was wondering . . ."

"David used to live there."

This time, it was David who exchanged smiles with their dining companion over Charley's interruption.

"I was *wondering*," David continued. "In what part of the city were you stationed?"

"Brooklyn."

"How'd you choose to become a firefighter?"

"One could say it chose me. Grew up in the life. Uncles and cousins, as well as my father. My mother insisted I graduate college, but I think she knew all along where I'd wind up. I tried other things but was in a firehouse before my twenty-fifth birthday."

Their meals arrived. Baskets with burgers, fries, and coleslaw, iced tea all around.

"Lew, may I offer a quick blessing?" Charley asked.

"If you don't, I will. So, please."

They held hands and bowed their heads.

"Lord, we ask you to bless this food before us, bless the hands that prepared it, bless those seated next to us, and bless the friendship between us."

"That was nice," Lew said. "And you said that better than any preacher I ever heard."

David nudged Charley. "Go ahead, *friend*. Show him your kryptonite."

"Kryptonite?" Lew asked.

Charley wrinkled her nose at David, then reached into her purse.

As David had done back in Kentucky, Lew slowly opened the leather-encased shield.

"Seattle. You're a long way from home. Chaplain?"

"Lew, I said much the same thing just a few days ago. Would you like to hear her story?"

Charley used one arm to reach for her shield and the other to direct a sharp elbow toward the man beside her.

"Yes, I would. It'll give me something to share with my Roberta at our evening meal. After over fifty years of marriage, my well of stimulating conversation often runs dry."

"I have a better idea. Let's have a conversation. My Aussie friend is welcome to join in at any time. He's a famous Hollywood screen-writer intent upon writing a book about my unremarkable life."

"Well, there's a story there as well, I imagine," Lew replied, with a wink, "but his will have to wait."

Charley decided, for her, brevity would be best.

"Lew, in one way, my path was similar to yours. My father and my husband were pastors. After seminary, my time was spent raising our daughter. When she went off to college, I became a social worker, then joined the police department."

The waitress stopped by to refresh their drinks and ask if the food was to their liking. All three assured her it was.

David sat quietly, anxious to hear the coming exchange.

"What was your training?" Lew asked..

"When the job was offered, I insisted on first going to the acade-my because . . . well, because I wanted to be *of them* and not just *with them*. So to speak."

"Them being the other cops."

"Of course."

"They were okay with that?" Lew asked.

Charley nodded.

"And you became just like other women officers?"

"Far, far from it. Same uniform, but that's where any similarity ended."

"Hope you don't mind my next question," Lew said. "Curiosity getting the best of me. Are you armed?"

Charley told Lew she was recently retired—without providing details. And without answering his question.

Charley and her Seattle employer experienced media exposure cutting both ways. The adverse publicity surrounding her ex-husband had engulfed her, ending the law enforcement career she'd loved and found so fulfilling. The department facilitated as graceful a departure as possible, and professional counseling was encouraged. She ignored the advice. Her priority was her daughter, and she tried everything possible to bring Rachel back into her life. Her heart broke when she received a "too little, too late" rebuff from the only person in the world she truly loved.

"I took the required weapons training," Charley told Lew. "But everyone knew they wouldn't ask me to carry something I'd never use. At graduation, several classmates gave me a bullet."

"I hope your colleagues in blue had the good sense not to make Barney Fife comparisons."

"A few did, but the joke got very old, very fast. Still, I always carried one of the bullets with me as a reminder of the danger we all faced every day."

David, remaining quiet, knew both were thinking of the fictional 1960s television town of Mayberry, where the folksy sheriff, Andy, didn't carry a gun. His cousin and only deputy, Barney, had an unloaded revolver on his belt but was allowed to keep one bullet in his shirt pocket.

Lew asked, "What were their expectations of you in that big police department?"

"I had a handbook to guide me, of course, but on day one, my supervisor told me I was on the payroll to assist other officers, not civilians. Plain, but far from simple."

"Did many of your fellow officers become your friends? And I do mean just friends, nothing more."

"I understand, Lew, and the answer is none. I didn't socialize with either men or women in any way at any time. There were times when we were together at off-duty gatherings, but since they were never really off-duty, neither was I."

"So, how did you go about building trust?"

"Patience and experience. I had to accept a slow process, one officer at a time. I was told—and I want to believe—there were times when I made a difference. That's what makes it—sorry, *made* it—all worthwhile."

David listened with rapt attention as Charley and Lew talked about the first responders they'd known and worked beside. His mind drifted to how he might write about them. No other domestic profession had members who got dressed every workday knowing the very nature of their duties meant it might be their last.

"Lew, except for the danger," David asked, "if you had to pick one thing that makes first responders different from other professions, what would it be?"

"I think about it this way. By the time most people retire, they've experienced the same year over and over again, say for twenty or thirty years. Maybe more. When first responders retire, they may have had as many years on the job, but most likely with no two days the same."

"And on that happy note," Charley said, "I vote we change subjects."

"Actually, folks, I need to be on my way. Time for my afternoon nap. Get cranky if I don't get it, and Roberta becomes less pleasant to live with. But after all this time, you'd think she'd be a bit more understanding." He smiled, adding, "Just kidding, of course." His eyes twinkled as he looked at Charley. "Mostly."

Charley and David rose when Lew pushed his chair back. They shook hands and watched him until he stopped their waitress near the front door. A few minutes later, the waitress brought their check.

David glanced at it. "This isn't right. Remember we asked you to add two other meals?"

"Yes, sir, I do. And I did."

"Then we owe you more. Four meals—ours and theirs."

"No sir, you don't. A nice older man told me to add your bill to his. I've seen this happen before. Not often, but it does happen."

David handed her cash for the first responders' meals and added a tip equal to that amount.

"Thank you!" The waitress beamed. "You folks travelin' the Route?"

"We are," Charley answered. She smiled at David. "All the way."

"I'm gonna do that myself someday. You drive careful, and may God be with you."

David had parked quite a ways from the restaurant entrance to avoid door bumps. As he and Charley walked across the gravel parking lot, two men climbed out of a battered pickup truck, the only vehicle anywhere close to Sheila. Charley's instincts took over when she touched her hand to David's arm.

They slowed their pace, and as they drew closer, they noticed each disheveled man had a tire iron in one hand. The younger of the two, bearded with long, stringy hair and looking to be in his late teens, walked a few steps over to the side of the Corvette and peered in the passenger-side window.

"Hey man, ain't this contraption got no cup holder?"

Even with a comfortable distance separating them, David's Australian accent was noticeable when he asked, "What is it you want?"

"A fer-a-ner. Derek. Look what we got here," he called back over his shoulder. "A fer-a-ner with a hot car *and* a hot babe."

"I'll ask again," David said, in a voice he hoped didn't reveal his growing discomfort. "What is it you want?"

Derek, also bearded, unkempt, and older than his companion by at least ten years, slouched against Sheila's boot and slapped his tire iron into an open palm. "Nothing much. Just all your money."

"And if we don't oblige you?" David asked.

"Oblige you? Listen to this shit," the younger man said.

"Me and Wilson ain't gonna harm you or the missus," the older man answered. "But won't say the same fer yer car."

"Yer choice," Wilson chimed in with a tire iron raised menacingly above Sheila. "All your money, and hers too, or we begin touching up this shiny paint job ya got here."

With utter calm and a firm voice, Charley told David, "I've got this."

She reached across to place her hand inside the purse hanging at the end of a strap on her left shoulder.

"The broad says she's got this, Derek. Reckon what else of his she's got in there besides money."

When Charley pulled her hand from the purse, David exclaimed, "Charley, don't!"

# 10

## "I've Got This."

Charley stepped away from David's side and strode purposefully toward Sheila and the two men, her running shoes steady on the gravel beneath them. At the end of an outstretched arm, her hand had a tight grip on a small handgun.

"Here's the deal, gentleman." Her confident voice reaffirmed the self-assurance her body language conveyed. "You're going to drop those tire irons to the ground in a way that won't damage our car. Then we—the three of us—are going to walk slowly, very slowly, over to your truck so I can make certain you don't have other weapons."

The men exchanged glances.

"Look at me!" she shouted. "Then you're going to drive away as fast as that thing will carry you in the opposite direction we're traveling. Which means," she said, her left arm pointing toward the east, "you go that way."

"And if'n we don't?" the younger man Wilson asked, cowering.

"My friend here will call 9-1-1, and we can take turns explaining an attempted armed robbery of a fellow police officer."

The older man's voice cracked with false bravado when he gestured toward David. "He ain't no cop."

David remembered Charley telling Lew she'd received police academy firearms training, and he could tell the men were far less sure of themselves than Charley appeared to be. He began to relax. Somewhat.

"That's right," David answered, "*she* is."

"Bullshit!" the younger man retorted as he took a step forward.

Charley didn't flinch. Her left shoulder dipped slightly. Her purse slipped off and fell to the ground, and she stopped them in their tracks when she brought her left hand up to the gun and stared them down.

She slowly waived her clasped hands back and forth, first toward one man, then the other.

"Here's the thing. We're in a bit of a hurry, and I'm all out of patience." She was close enough to know that fear and days without bathing combined to give both men the dank aroma of an unwashed gym towel. "I'm going to count to five before my friend behind me makes the call. Your choice. One!"

Charley and David watched as the pickup truck churned up a cloud of dust and loudly sped off in an easterly direction. Only then did Charley return the gun to her purse.

David hadn't moved. When they both came alongside Sheila, he said, "Please explain to me what just happened."

Charley told him that while she hadn't carried a weapon on the job, she had kept up with the annual training and had a universal concealed carry permit.

"Because?"

"*Because* of the death threats that came my way from my ex-husband's troubles."

"Is it loaded now?"

"It is."

"If they'd come at us, would you have shot at them?"

"No, I was going to throw it at one of them and hope it scared both of them away."

"I'm being serious. You *really* would have shot one or both of them?"

"I would," she answered evenly. "If we had no other choice."

"What about running back to the restaurant?"

*I'm all done running.*

"And leave Sheila defenseless? I think not."

"Okay, then, why didn't we call 911?"

"Didn't need to."

The last thing Charley wanted was to be named in a police report that would find its way into a database accessible by Seattle authorities. "Isn't that a bit . . . what's the word I'm looking for? Oh, yes, incongruous. You know. What you told Lew a few minutes ago. About clergy and handguns."

"I choose to think of it as situational. Kinda like how surgery might alter one's perspective on narcotics."

David started to speak. Charley held up her hand. "And no, we're not going to delve any further. What's done is done. Let's get going."

David opened the passenger door.

"An entirely new side of Charley Chaplain," he muttered

Charley fastened her seat belt and with the door still open, said, "What can I say? Like an onion. Peeling layers. You okay to drive?"

They rode in silence for several miles.

"Well, that was certainly something. In all the excitement, I forgot to thank you. Thank you."

"You're welcome. Let's not talk about it anymore. Okay?"

"Okay. Let's talk about our wonderful lunch with Lew. I understand why both of you did what you did with the checks. Something I'm going to try to remember from now on."

"Can't speak for Lew, but I do it every chance I get. People like those two don't earn anywhere near what they should. We often hear people say 'thank you for your service' to people who served in the military, and we should. But never, or almost never, do we say it to first responders in uniform. And we should."

Ten more miles down the road before Charley spoke again.

"Say, David, can you answer that man's question?"

"What question was that?"

"For over a hundred thousand dollars, why doesn't a Corvette have cup holders?"

"I thought you didn't want to talk about our little encounter with the local gentry."

"My question wasn't about them. It was about Sheila."

David kept his left hand on the steering wheel while his right hand pressed down on the back portion of the center console. It retracted, revealing two cup holders.

"You mean these?"

"Nicely played," she acknowledged.

"I thought so."

With sun-kissed blue skies above them and a beaten-down road beneath them, they continued on in Illinois until a brief stop an hour later in Springfield, the final resting place for Abraham Lincoln. But as David had cautioned back in Bowling Green, there'd be no time for sightseeing.

Onward they went, through small towns and even smaller hamlets, each strewn with a smattering of dilapidated buildings decaying under sloped roofs one good windstorm away from collapse. The last vestiges of a once prosperous time in out-of-the-way places during a bygone era of American wanderlust.

They rode along, lost in their own thoughts, though David was anxious to re-open a previous conversation. He broke the silence.

"We've agreed a book isn't going to happen."

*The wind-up*, she thought.

"That we did," she replied, hesitantly.

"We've got several days ahead of us to fill with conversation, so I was wondering . . ."

*The pitch.*

". . . since you left your career completely out of telling me your story, would you mind if we talked about the conversation you had with Lew?"

"Yes."

"Yes we can talk about it, or yes, you'd mind?"

David's peripheral vision settled on her arms firmly intertwined across her chest, wordlessly conveying her thoughts. He'd anticipated as much.

"Here's an idea. What if we barter? You share, and in turn, I'll regale you with an obscene amount of Hollywood gossip."

"Hmm. The gossip angle from a true Hollywood insider is certainly enticing." After several seconds of silent pondering, she firmly said, "No."

*Oh, well,* he thought. *So much for that gambit.*

The directions David's GPS laid out for them mostly paralleled Interstate 55. In a couple of places, Route 66 was so degraded that they surfed on and off the interstate for several miles at a time. According to the travel guide Charley was now reading, it would happen many times before they reached their evening destination. After a long quiet spell, she set the guide on the floor.

"Question for you. If you didn't know anything about my career until today, why were you so certain from talking with Marla Jo that a book was out of the question?"

He told her that in his only conversation with Marla Jo, she hadn't given him enough to have an opinion. "But listening to you today, I now wonder . . ."

"Still not gonna happen."

"I don't mean with me. I'm thinking of either Marla Jo or Ben."

"Doesn't change my answer. Oh, and it's nap time. Me, not you."

They'd reached the impasse Charley would reference early in the following year when she delivered a speech from the ballroom stage in a downtown Seattle hotel.

David could tell from the relaxed rhythm of her breathing that she'd fallen asleep almost as soon as she'd closed her eyes. He drove through one small town after the other, continuously dismayed at how many buildings had been allowed to atrophy and die, their life gone but the outer shell remaining—not unlike the route itself in so many places.

Charley woke and stretched. "After all the day's excitement, do you need to pull over somewhere and get yourself some rest?"

"No, I'm fine. We're not that far from quittin' time in St. Louis."

Charley looked at the travel guide map with mile markers for destinations from one end of Route 66 to the other. She had not expected to reach their California destination in time for her to meet her Friday deadline two states to the north. Now she knew for certain they would not and was surprised at how unconcerned she was with the realization she'd become a fugitive in a few days. When she didn't turn herself in on time, there were plenty of resources to find her—if she chose to stay alive that long. For now, she was determined to cast those thoughts aside and keep her mind on the time she would have with David.

It was late afternoon when they crossed the Mississippi River and arrived at St. Louis. David handed over the keys to the valet parking attendant, and they effortlessly repeated the same luxury hotel registration as the night before in Chicago.

As they walked toward the elevators, Charley said, "Your second day with your new car and your first on the fabled highway. Thoughts?"

"I think we've both fared rather well, don't you? Except for that encounter at the truck stop."

"I agree. Hungry?"

David told Charley the trip had exhausted him and asked to "beg off" having dinner together.

Though she wanted as much time with him as possible, she answered, "Not a problem."

"I'm certain without looking they have a great room service menu if you don't want to dine alone in the restaurant."

The elevator doors opened.

"Tell the truth. You don't want me sitting alone so a handsome stranger, such as yourself, can approach me with an insipid pickup line like, oh, I don't know, something like 'You look a bit lonely over there.'"

"Worked at JAR's Pub, didn't it?"

The doors closed.

"No, it didn't. I wouldn't be here, and none of this would be happening, if Marla Jo hadn't roped us both into a greasy spoon breakfast the next morning."

She pushed the buttons for their respective rooms.

He grinned. "I'm gonna tell Karen what you said about her Kastle."

"And just how are you going to do that? Planning on a return visit anytime soon?"

"Okay, I guess I won't. Back to the present. You sure you're okay dining alone . . . wherever you decide to be alone?"

"Of course. Don't worry about me. I'll just charge everything to your room."

"Did I say I was paying for *everything*?"

"David Jacobs, you're impossible!"

"Been called worse."

"I have no doubt."

The doors opened to Charley's floor.

"Say," she continued, "you were awfully quiet at times this afternoon. Whatcha thinkin'?"

"I have an idea. Happens from time to time. Less now than before."

"Not back on the book, I hope."

He shook his head.

"What, then?"

David pressed the button to keep the door open.

"Not fully formed. Be assured you'll be the first to hear all about it. And with that, I'm going to call it a day. But not without thanking you again for coming with me. And rescuing us from the bad guys."

"My pleasure. See you in the morning. Sleep well."

As the door closed with Charley still in view, David knew he'd always remember her words: "I've got this."

# 11

## *Top Gun*

**W**hen they met in the opulent lobby the next morning, each had made only the slightest tweaks to their attire. Since David had assured Charley every hotel they stayed at would offer one-hour laundry and dry-cleaning services, Charley had repeatedly declined David's offer to outfit them with the Route 66 memorabilia clothing displayed at each stop.

"How was your evening?" David asked.

"Pretty interesting. In the bar, I met a handsome man who swept me off my feet, and we were together for an evening of dining and dancing all around St. Louis. You?"

"Much the same. Picked at my room service dinner while pecking away at my computer, then lights out."

"Picking and pecking," she echoed. "Well, you know *I'm* not telling the truth."

"I am. Wanted to get some thoughts down before losing them in the abyss of short-term memory loss. Another side effect of my meds."

Charley had become adept at recognizing conversational bread-crumbs he dropped, hoping she'd take a nibble.

"Well, is it?"

"Is what?"

"Your idea from last night. Were you and your computer able to fully form it?"

"You remembered. I'm impressed."

"And?"

"Best described as half-baked."

"I see. May I at least know what's in the oven?"

"I'd really only feel comfortable sharing with a friend. Are we there yet?"

She smiled, remembering his Karen's Kastle comment about wanting to become more than friends. *Hard to believe that was such a short time ago.*

"Getting there, I think," she answered.

"Me, too. Now, please hear me out before you say anything."

"Ooo-kay."

David served up an uninspired suggestion that Charley work with either or both Taylors as ghostwriters of her story. He did it to get a *no* out of the way before sharing what he really had in mind. The calculated no-then-yes had worked beautifully in one of his Hollywood scripts, and he hoped the same could be true now.

"My turn to talk?" she asked.

"Yes."

"No."

"Not surprised. What I expected. And I promise I won't mention it again."

"Good. That it?"

He shook his head.

"You have my attention. Or will have over breakfast."

Seated in the hotel restaurant that fairly shouted "expensive" with its chandeliers, white tablecloths, and tuxedoed waiters, David proposed the idea of a magazine article, perhaps a series of articles, about first responders. He explained he drew inspiration from the paramedics and the firefighter they'd met the day before in McLean. He also recalled the late '80s movie *Top Gun* emerged from a single article in a California magazine.

David paused when a breakfast that didn't faintly resemble anything on the Karen's Kastle menu was placed before them. The imperious waiter departed, allowing Charley to observe that, despite the exorbitant prices, less must be considered more.

David let her observation go unchallenged and picked up where he'd left off.

"Not thinking of a movie, of course. Would something like what I'm suggesting be remotely within the realm of possibility?"

"Possibly."

David smiled with a sense of accomplishment.

The smile faded when Charley added, "Where do I fit in?"

"I thought we agreed you didn't. And neither does anything you saw or experienced."

Charley spooned berries from one small bowl into a pint-sized bowl of yogurt. "I'm confused. How will this work?"

"Thinking out loud here."

David described the evening he'd spent compiling thoughts on his computer and doing online research.

"I could write a first draft while getting treatment, then send it for your thoughts. You could even come to Oregon, and we could work on it together. After all, only one of us has written a bestselling book."

A small frown line crept between her eyes, then disappeared. At that moment, she was still uncertain she'd return to Seattle, and if she did go, she'd be in the King County jail or confined to house arrest. Oregon was out of the question.

"I wrote that book when I was too young and stupid to know any better. Thank you, but no encore from this girl."

David took solace in his expectation they would still have several more days together. "Just think it over. Please. That's all I'm asking. We can leave the idea alone, for now, and talk about it again closer to Santa Monica. And if you agree, when we're finished writing, we'll send our final draft to Marla Jo to polish, and you'll have the final say-so before she tries to get it published."

The more David talked, the more resolute Charley became. But she didn't want a dampening of his enthusiasm to come between them. "How about I go this far with you today? I'll call Marla Jo for her opinion, then give you mine."

"Only fair. More than fair."

They both finished every bite of their modest-sized breakfasts and were still hungry, but neither showed any inclination to delay their departure.

"Ready to go?" David asked. "The other Sheila is waiting and anxious to stretch her legs."

As he drove away, he said, "You haven't asked, but our overnight destination is another Springfield. Missouri this time. Queen City of the Ozarks."

In their early departure, both quietly reflected on David's idea. What he'd articulated was a dicey proposition, at best. He had no firm idea what things would be like while getting treatment—and after. Charley still had no idea the seriousness of her traveling companion's condition, but what she did know was her ability to communicate while behind bars would be limited. If she accepted that fate, which was becoming more and more unlikely in her mind. Yet neither was prepared to accept the reality truthfulness would bring.

Charley was engrossed in the travel guide, and with St. Louis miles behind them, she didn't recognize the name of a single town along the day's planned travel as Route 66 at times paralleled I-44 in a southwesterly direction. And in many instances, the two roads converged for short distances. Unless something unforeseen occurred, as the previous day had shown entirely possible, Sheila's GPS had them arriving in Springfield around four in the afternoon.

Although Marla Jo had been the one to orchestrate their breakfast meeting three days earlier, they'd impulsively thrown themselves together in a way that meant they'd be alone with no one else around, friend or stranger, for long periods of time. Each had grown increasingly comfortable with the synchrony between them, and the morning quiet in the car seemed nothing but ordinary.

David's curiosity about Charley's "well-rounded" life and unique career had been more than satisfied, except for one thing. The circumstances of her ex-husband's death, something Charley had yet to expound upon. For now, his magazine idea gave him something far better to silently contemplate than how imperiled *his* life had become over the past year. In the company of such a beautiful and intriguing woman, not to mention bantering peer and subduer of scoundrels, he felt happy for the first time since his diagnosis.

In the car's quietude, Charley found herself gazing at the passing scenery while continuing to relive her not-so-distant past. Much of her adult life before chaplainship had been lived without passion or purpose, leading to depression and occasional suicidal thoughts. Her daughter's presence and the certainty of their unbreakable bond had always shoved those horrible thoughts aside. But when Rachel went off to college, and their relationship grew strained, Charley had nothing to fill the emptiness in her days. Ending it all by her own hand seemed increasingly more enticing than the slow death of a thousand indignities imposed by keeping up appearances as merely a trophy on her famous husband's public shelf. It seemed enticing now, too, as she faced the inevitability of incarceration for something she hadn't done but doubted anyone would believe.

David asked Charley what held her in such deep contemplation. When she didn't answer, he went fishing.

"Any regrets about coming along?"

"No, not at all. Just thinking about things. And one of those things was your promise to . . . how did you put it exactly? Oh yes, regale me with Hollywood gossip. You even seasoned the offer with the word obscene."

David had prided himself on never once doing what he'd too hastily served up to tantalize Charley.

"I did say that, didn't I?"

"Uh, huh, you did."

"I'll need some time to get my thoughts together," he answered, tripping over his words. "To cull out the truly salacious things that might offend your gracious sensibilities."

"Gracious? Did you say gracious?"

"If I'm not mistaken, it's the word you used to describe yourself as a traveling companion when we were but minutes into our journey. Wouldn't want to offend."

"Ever the exasperating Aussie. And we both know you're stalling to run out our clock and walk back a promise made just so you could poke around into *my* life. Is there an Australian word for someone who would do such a thing to someone like, well, me for instance?"

David quickly sorted through a slang repertoire he knew but seldom deployed.

"Galah."

"Which means?"

"Fool."

"Sums it up nicely. Thank you for that. Now, to demonstrate my *graciousness*, I'll try my best to be patient while you gather your thoughts. You can begin with the Sheila that you followed to America. Deal?"

"What else can I say but deal? I'll make good on my promise once we reach Texas."

"And I'll hold you to it. But just one question—for now. I've seen a lot of your Hollywood Sheila's movies. The one who dumped you. She sure does cry a lot."

"Comes from remembering her time with me," he deadpanned.

"Only you would know. Seriously, I've often wondered how actors can cry when the scene calls for it."

"Many, not her, can dig deep and find the emotion that leads to tears."

"And other actors, like her?"

"More simple than you might think. A makeup person uses a tube to blow the aroma of camphor into their face."

"Wonders never cease."

<hr />

They stopped at Devil's Elbow for fuel and a quick but satisfying lunch. The tiny village was known for its idyllic, river-bluff scenery, and the travel guide suggested taking time for a stroll across an abandoned steel-truss bridge overlooking a river. Walking side by side, they both had a sense of closeness without touching. And neither felt the compulsion to talk.

Above them, a cloudless Cerulean sky, as blue and as vast as any ocean. Away from roads and highways that had so dominated their senses the past few days, the silence broken only by the wind rustling through the trees and the scraping of dead leaves cartwheeling across the wooden bridge. Unseen birds chirped from branches scattered among the trees. The trail sloped down to a rapidly-moving shallow stream that gurgled noisily as it passed over rocks and tree debris. Up the shoreline, but easily visible, a pair of beavers were hard at work.

"This is a truly glorious place, isn't it?" Charley asked.

"That it is."

They relished the quiet that blanketed the area before sauntering back to the car and heading down the road.

Charley opened the travel guide. "We've taken time to stretch our legs, and this morning you said something about stretching Sheila's. It looks like there's a lot of interstate running parallel to Route 66 after we leave Springfield tomorrow morning."

"Tempting as it might be, my vision in the one eye isn't what it should be. And the meds I'm taking shouldn't be mixed with reckless driving, even for a short distance. You, however, a kryptonite-bearing retired law enforcement-type person, are most welcome to take the wheel tomorrow."

*The man never quits.*

"As I've heard it said, the chances of that are slim and none, and slim didn't make the trip."

At that moment, David swerved to avoid a gaping pothole.

"Well done! Mario Andretti couldn't have done it better."

"Oh, if only the flattery were sincere. But I'll keep trying to be worthy."

"I have no doubt." She paused. "While we walked on the bridge, it occurred to me that we may have told each other everything worth knowing about ourselves." *Or at least what I'm willing to tell.*

"Is that a problem?" he asked, her ex's death still on his mind.

"Could be. We've got several more days ahead, and we've already done our walks down memory lane."

"Or—"

"Or what?" she countered.

"Or we could be making new memories. All in how one looks at it."

"You know, David, you should consider becoming a writer."

"I'll do just that. And here's a thought. Can you think of anything, anything at all, you've not told me that you think I might find interesting? Emphasis on interesting, not necessarily juicy."

*If he only knew how much I've left out.*

*If she only knew how much I've left out.*

"Okay, you might find this interesting. My daughter Rachel's husband is Jewish."

"No kidding? How's that for coincidence?"

"Oh, the coincidence goes a little bit deeper. His name is—"

"Don't tell me! David?"

"How 'bout that? You said you were open to new character ideas for your movies. A Jewish man and Christian woman. At least, I think Rachel still regards herself as Christian. Hope so."

"Good idea, but it's been done. Incredibly well, I might add."

She reflected on some of the movies David shared he'd had a part in.

"Was it a crime thriller?"

"Love story."

Coming on the heels of David's "making new memories" comment, those two words gave each of them pause.

"*The Way We Were*," David continued. "Jewish political activist, played by Barbra Streisand. Robert Redford was her WASPish apolitical lover who became her husband."

"I've seen it several times, but religion wasn't really a big part of the story, was it?"

"True. Barely mentioned."

"You know what I find especially interesting?" she asked.

"That it was the woman who was Jewish?"

"No. That the man was a Hollywood screenwriter. And in the end, they weren't a good match. They had a daughter, coincidently named Rachel, and got divorced. Like me."

"Art imitating life, as they say, but it wasn't religion that doomed them. It was politics. A subject that has yet to rear its ugly head with us."

"May it never."

"Charley, you said you weren't certain if Rachel still regarded herself as a Christian. How troubling is that for you?"

Their first dinner together, they'd agreed both politics and religion were off-limits. With politics consigned to the trash bin a moment earlier, Charley's slow response prepared David for pushback. She surprised him.

"The easy answer, the one you're probably expecting, is that it would trouble me greatly. I've thought a lot about it, and the truth is, it doesn't. I did all I could for Rachel while she was growing up, and now I have no influence in her life whatsoever. In fact, I'm not even *in* her life. All of that saddens me, but it's her decision. One we both have to live with."

"And you? How are you feeling about such things these days?"

"Give the man an inch, and he –"

"Sorry. I know what we agreed, and I transgressed."

"I don't mind. Thought a lot about that, too. With all the crap that's happened to me the past few months that I don't deserve, it's as if the guard rails for the religion I've relied upon since childhood are gone. To make matters worse, I can't even see the road ahead."

"About your road ahead. From all you've shared and getting to know you, I can easily understand why your late ex's book was a best-seller. You should consider returning to the keyboard again."

"You never give up, do you?"

"Not easily."

"Well, then, I just might think about it." Even though she knew she wouldn't. "And just so you know, I've been thinking about your magazine article idea, and I think I may be okay with it."

Surprised by her change of heart, he rushed a reply. "That's great! And it'll keep us connected after our trip is over. Means a lot."

"Not so fast. I still need to talk with Marla Jo. Hear what she has to say." Charley saw the disappointment in his face. "Even thought of a name. What about *Hearts Beneath Their Shields?*"

A smile erased his despondency. "The perfect title. Well done. Well done, *indeed.*"

"Aw, don't you just say the nicest things."

"I was being completely serious. And I can't help feeling you're mocking me."

"You were . . . and I was. Just tryin' ta keep things light and lively."

From Phillipsburg south of Devil's Elbow, Main Street USA meandered a fair distance from the interstate almost all the way to their overnight destination. They arrived in their second Springfield of the day well within the time constraints of "happy hour." After checking into the hotel and receiving assurances that David's car would be well cared for, they accepted the concierge's suggestion and walked across the street to a local bar.

The tavern reminded them of the pub where they first met. About the same size and windowless. Booths lining one wall, tables and chairs scattered about. A ten-stool bar. One big difference: a juke box and a small dance floor.

They settled at a corner table, a beer for David and a glass of house wine for Charley.

David raised his glass. "I understand some religious folks have a problem with alcohol, even in social settings. Glad you're not one of them."

Charley lifted her glass. "Jesus's first miracle was turning water into wine. At a party, no less."

"You're making that up."

She set her glass down, reached into her purse, and withdrew a small paperback. She expertly thumbed to a page and pointed to a passage.

"Read."

It took less than thirty seconds in the second chapter of John before David handed back a well-worn copy of the New Testament.

"Interesting," he said. "A Bible and a handgun nestled against each other in your purse. I would have thought—"

"David, I don't mean to be unkind, but not every thought we have needs to be spoken."

He realized he'd gone where he shouldn't have and apologized profusely.

"Apology accepted. But please promise me that's the last I'll hear of that layer of my onion peeled back in front of you."

"I promise. And again, I'm sorry."

*Things need to go a different direction.* "David, we always seem to be talking about me a lot more than you. Since you're the one who brought up religion, what about you?"

"What do you mean? What about me?"

"Okay. Simple question. Do you regard yourself as more faithful than religious, which is where I'm at right now in my life, or the other way around?"

"Haven't been asked that. I suppose the truth is, sitting here to-night, more faithful than religious is probably a fair statement."

David shared he'd stopped actively practicing his faith decades earlier when he arrived in New York with a woman who was neither faithful nor religious, but he had found himself lately back on the path. He didn't offer more, and she didn't ask.

"Well, I hope God will have Her hand on your shoulder."

He could have let that pass by but didn't.

"David, this could be an extremely long discussion, one you and I are not going to have. I'm not bound to one certain imagery, one gender, when I think about God, speak about God, and pray to Her."

He started to speak, she raised her hand. "Enough. For now, at least. Please."

"Agreed. Question for you. Unrelated. Bar food here or fine cuisine elsewhere?"

A half-hour later, they were nearing the end of a delicious serving of homemade burgers and fries, a selection becoming standard Route 66 fare for them.

"Don't mind if I do," David said, lifting one of several fries remaining on her plate after she set it aside.

She watched him and casually said, "I have a request."

"Anything."

"Dance with me."

His lack of enthusiasm was apparent as he eyed the jukebox as if it were a coiled snake about to do him great harm. "As long as it's something slow so I won't embarrass both of us."

She rested her elbow on the table and extended her arm. "Do you have any quarters?"

Charley walked across the empty dance floor, studied the jukebox for the longest time, then returned to lead David by the hand to the edge of the dance floor.

"What took you so long to decide?" he asked. "Looking for something in particular?"

"You'll see."

She leaned into his arms, and they began slow dancing to Barbra Streisand singing the title song to a familiar movie.

Several slow country music favorites chosen by David and Charley were interspersed with faster tunes selected by other revelers. David and Charley sat those out. An hour later, they walked back across the street and noticed Sheila had been placed in a secure spot straddling two spaces just to the right of the main entrance.

*Great advertising for the hotel*, David thought.

Charley ran her finger across the car's roofline as they passed by. She turned around to look again as they reached the door being held open by a uniformed bellman.

"Penny for your thoughts," David said.

He made a show of searching his pockets.

"At least a quarter," she said.

"It appears mine are all in the juke box."

They stood silently for a moment; he spoke first. "Your turn."

"Oh, that. Nothing much." She gestured toward his car. "Just thinking about getting one of these for myself."

"Really? I'm surprised. More than."

"Wouldn't be any more out of place than everything else in my life seems to be." *Except you.*

"Maybe I just give you mine."

The idea had come to him a split second before he spoke, and it was something he could make happen with the greatest of ease—and pleasure. Just thinking about it warmed him.

"Yeah, sure. And right after that, the Seattle Mariners win the World Series."

"Don't be so quick to doubt. And with the colors you don't think are befitting a Sheila, you could even rename it Bruce."

As they walked through the lobby toward the elevators, David reached to take her hand.

"David, I think we *are* becoming friends."

"Better, I think."

After they said good-night and went to their separate rooms, the promised phone call was placed to Marla Jo, whose enthusiasm for the magazine article was less than David's but more than Charley's.

"I'll happily look at anything David sends me," Marla Jo said. "Other than that, how's it all going?" She listened to Charley's lengthy recital. "Sounds to me like you're falling in love with him.

Are you?"

Though surprised by the question, Charley felt she was on the cusp of a newly reimagined life. "I don't know. Maybe I am. Is it possible for that to happen in only three days?"

"I believe it is. More easily in books and movies, but certainly in real life. Do you think David knows how you feel?"

"I haven't said anything, so he'd have no way of knowing."

Marla Jo had known David for years, known him well, worked with him as he put feelings into words for fictional characters leading imaginary lives in make-believe worlds. She was certain David was far from unaware but kept that thought to herself.

"Are you going to tell him?" she asked.

"What's the point? I mean, we're together now, but in a few more days, we'll be gone from each other, probably forever."

"Maybe, maybe not. Forever might not be as long as either of you think."

Charley carried that sliver of Marla Jo's optimism with her as she fell asleep.

# 12

# *More Than Just Friends*

The spacious hotel lobby had a nouveau riche ambience chosen by an owner who had recently come into unexpected wealth, but good taste hadn't yet caught up. Whatever they were trying to achieve, they missed by a country mile.

The next morning, as Charley and David sat in overstuffed arm chairs that seemed as mismatched and out of place as the rest of the inelegant décor, she whispered under her breath that perhaps the owner, the decorator, or both, were color-blind.

"Or this was all designed by a committee," he answered in a whisper, "with each member allowed at least one independent decision."

They decided to have breakfast in a more appealing environment somewhere else. Before driving away, David studied the travel guide and saw an uninterrupted stretch of Route 66 all the way to Joplin, seventy miles away. As he drove, Charley scoured the guide and suggested their best chance for a satisfying breakfast might be in Carthage, about twenty miles shy of Joplin.

Their southwesterly morning drive took them past richly tim-
bered landscapes interspersed with fertile bottom lands, and for the
first time, windows down, fresh air rushing in. An hour later, they
arrived at Carthage, a thriving agricultural community. To their de-
light, they spotted a quaint diner on the town's main drag at the first
stoplight intersection. Once inside, the spotless eatery appeared, to
them, virtually unchanged for decades. They found the breakfast fare
delicious, and David remarked the excellent food and modest prices
were a welcome throwback to another time on the Mother Road.

Back in Sheila, David asked to look at the guide.

"All those zigs and zags after we leave Joplin make it look like
the chart of an up-and-down company on the stock exchange," he
said. "But it could be fun."

"Nothing wrong with fun," Charley said, as they pulled away
from the restaurant, her mind on something far more important to
her than the peculiarities of the road ahead.

Their Kansas fun lasted all of twelve miles from the time they
entered the state just north of Joplin until they crossed over into
Oklahoma, heading back in a southerly direction.

*No wonder Kansas was the only Route 66 state I couldn't remember,*
David thought.

Hours later, they were about halfway to their end-of-day
Tulsa destination when Charley couldn't withhold her question a
moment longer.

"David, yesterday when I said I thought we really were becoming friends, you said 'better.' What did you mean?" She waited what felt like a reasonable interlude. "Didn't think that was a
difficult question."

David knew how his feelings for her had evolved and vacillated
between shading a reply with nuance or sending it straight over the
net. What had begun as a mere inkling after they left Chicago had
grown from infatuation to love by the time they'd reached the dance

floor. He'd begun looking ahead in life with optimism and enthusiasm and stopped thinking about death and dying.

The car's compact interior closed in on him, and he went with nuance, hoping the same feelings were also stirring inside her.

"I thought I was in love once . . . and probably was. I've been *in like* with several women, though far fewer than many of my Hollywood mates. There's only been one woman I've considered just a close friend, and she's married to Ben."

"All well and good, but where does that leave me?" she asked impatiently.

"Before some things happened yesterday, I would have said *like*. Different from my friendship with Marla Jo, and since we haven't been, shall we say, intimate, different from all the others."

"What things?"

"When I held you in my arms on the dance floor, and when I laid awake for hours, thinking about the past few days with the most remarkable woman I've ever known."

Charley's chin quivered as she reached over and put her hand on his arm.

"Well, those few words took my breath away."

"And they weren't big ones."

"They didn't need to be."

"Left one out, though." He waited until he could safely take his eyes of the road for a second or two to look at her. "Love."

She squeezed his arm. "Please don't think of this as competition, but I got across that finish line ahead of you."

"Sorry, if this *were* competition, I'd win."

She laughed softly. "Last night I told Marla Jo."

"Were you waiting for *her* to tell me?"

"No, of course not!"

Charley withdrew into herself but didn't withdraw her hand from David's arm.

His words broke her spell. "Well, we've solved one problem."

She turned toward him. "What problem?"

"Running out of things to talk about. Now we have heaps."

"Heaps?"

"Aussie-speak for plenty."

"Heaps, huh? Okay, you lead, I'll follow."

"Not a problem. Since you told her before me, may I ask about your talk with Marla Jo?"

"Oh, it was mostly me telling her about our trip and talking a lot about you. She asked if I was falling in love."

"To which you . . .?"

"Asked if such a thing was even possible in such a short time. She told me the two of you have made it happen many times in fiction, so why not in real life?"

"What she said is true. About our writing, that is."

"Any others you can think of? By other writers."

"Give me a moment." He paused for several seconds, then continued. "Certainly Eric Segal with *Love Story* in the late sixties. Robert James Waller with *Bridges of Madison County* sometime in the eighties." Another pause. "More recently, Nicholas Sparks with *Nights in Rodanthe*. All made into very successful movies, I might add."

"Interesting. Now maybe you have a book about me that I'll agree to. On second thought, nah."

David told her it was her turn.

"No wokkas. Totally up for it."

"No wokkas, no worries. Been studying up on Down Under slang, have we?"

"Can't beat 'em, join 'em. Now, if I had to bet, it would be that about most things, especially material ones, you're a minimalist. Would I be right?"

David nodded.

126

"You said I should lead a conversation. I can't hear your head move."

He turned in her direction. "Yes, officer, I confess to being a minimalist. Is that a crime?"

"Eyes on the road, if you please. And to spare you the burden of asking, I'm the polar opposite."

"Opposite have been known to attract."

"Oh, I think we're doing okay so far. Here's another."

They quickly discovered their taste in music was anything but similar. Contemporary and country for Charley; blues and jazz for David. They found common ground with Keith Urban, the country singer from Australia, long-retired ABBA from Sweden, and the late chart-crossing eighties superstar John Denver.

"Do you realize we haven't once had the radio on. Does this thing have one?"

"You risk offending Sheila by calling her a *thing*. But, yes. Satellite radio. We can dial-up just about anything we want."

"Let's begin with John Denver. What's your favorite?"

He thought for a moment. "Toss-up. *Rocky Mountain High* or *Take Me Home Country Roads*."

David pulled into the parking lot of a roadside café where he could safely study the owner's manual to activate the entertainment system with the touch-pad display.

Underway again, they listened first to *Country Roads*, then his second choice. Hearing Denver singing about a man in his fifty-seventh year, Charley waited until the song ended.

"Fifty-seven. Is that about how old you are?"

"Good guess. Will be on my next birthday. October."

"Since I know you're going to ask, I'm fifty-three. My birthday is next month."

"If I'm still there, you can come to Oregon and we can celebrate."

*Celebrating my birthday with my newfound love. How wonderful that would be.*

"I'll think about it," she replied. "If I do, cake and candles, if you please."

"You bet. Want me to leave the radio on?"

Charley welcomed the opportunity to be alone with her thoughts. "That would be nice, if you don't mind."

"Don't mind at all."

Music replaced conversation for the better part of an hour. Charley's thoughts careened back and forth between dreaming about the life she now wanted and the reality it could never be. The unfairness overwhelmed her, but she succeeded in suppressing tears.

They stopped at Chelsea, and Charley stood beside David at the gas pump.

"The book says we've put almost two hundred miles between Springfield and here," she said.

"Making good time, don't you think?" he asked.

"No argument there. It's just that we got so wrapped up talking about minimalism and music and—"

"Falling in love?"

"That, too. It's just that we forgot about lunch."

At the small café recommended by two locals sitting in rocking chairs in front of the gas station, the lone waitress told them fried chicken was the house specialty.

"Sounds good." David looked at Charley. "Make that for two, please."

The waitress called out their order to the cook who was but a few steps away. Both Charley and David noticed the spelling of her name on her uniform: Sioux-Z.

And she noticed them noticing.

"Changed it when I was old enough to do it without my parent's permission But they're kinda okay with it because it still sounds the same."

"Is it because of your heritage?"

"Yeah. Might not be able to tell by lookin' at me, but my mother's mother's mother was a full-blooded Sioux. Lived in the Black Hills of South Dakota. That's a real sacred place for our nation. That's why I did it."

"That's wonderful," Charley said, "and different. And if I may say, you're very beautiful."

"No one's ever said that to me," she replied, overcome with shyness. "No one. Thank you."

At that moment, the cook dropped his palm on a bell.

"And I'm gonna move to South Dakota someday," the waitress said.

"Because of your ancestors?" David asked.

She nodded. "And because I want to live someplace special, close to nature, where weather's the only authority in my life."

Sioux-Z reached to lift both plates off the counter separating the kitchen from the eating area.

"It's such a nice day," she told them. "Would you like to eat outside? There's a picnic table out back under a shade tree just made for the two of you."

"Dining in the outback would be perfect. Wouldn't it, David?"

David directed, "Clever," toward Charley, then turned to Sioux-Z. "That would be great."

Charley's smile grew when she saw him give the young woman a hundred-dollar bill and tell her to keep the change.

"Outback. That really *was* clever," David admitted when they were seated side-by-side at the picnic table. "But with me, you only have an audience of one. Should think seriously about becoming a writer."

"Kind of you to say . . . again. And again. And again. But I'll cede that ground to you and Marla Jo and content myself with becoming your biggest fan. Hers, too. Oh, and Ben."

David reached to put his arm around Charley's waist, and she rested her head on his shoulder. They heard excited sounds of children playing in a nearby school yard, and a clock in the steeple rising above a church across the street struck three times. The setting was picture-perfect for a leisurely middle-of-the-afternoon picnic on a balmy April afternoon along America's Highway.

"This is a happy place," Charley said. "Like the end of a rainbow."

David gave her shoulder a confirming hug before sliding off the bench to return their plates, wrappings, and utensils. Their waitress looked up from the magazine she was reading when he asked if there was anything she thought they might find interesting to stop and see between there and Tulsa.

David responded to her enthusiastic suggestion with, "I'm glad I asked. Thank you."

Sioux-Z walked out the door with him to say goodbye.

"Travel safely," she said. "Be well and happy."

Claremore was midway between Chelsea and Tulsa. They detoured for their second brief sightseeing diversion to the Will Rogers Memorial. The stone edifice sat on twenty acres of land Rogers had purchased in 1911 as a future retirement home, but his death in 1935 in an Alaska plane crash kept him from fulfilling his plan. His widow created the museum and gardens in his memory.

As they approached the Tulsa city limits, a question from Charley. "Who's your favorite author?"

"Have to think about it." And he did. "Back in New York, an easy answer. Andrew Greeley. A Chicago priest no longer with us. He wrote dozens of novels with real-life intrigue, crime, romance. Even sordid things like infidelity and murder. But his protagonists were all in some way or the other tied to the Catholic faith."

"And now?"

"Because of what I do, Neil Simon is in a category all alone. His dialogue is second to none."

"Is that what your novels will be like?"

"You can't be successful with stage plays and screenplays unless you've got a talent for dialogue. I have a tiny bit. Mac does all the heavy lifting. We both know the ingredients, but he comes up with the recipe."

"Wrapping oneself once more in the cloak of understatement, are we?" she asked.

He shrugged.

"Well, I've come to know you're not very effusive about yourself. I kind of like that about you. But David, please don't restrain yourself when thinking or speaking about me."

"And so it shall be," he answered, with a smile.

They checked into the Hardrock Casino Hotel owned by the Cherokee Nation in the Tulsa suburb of Catoosa. On-property dining options ranged from gourmet fare to a Route 66-themed café.

"I can go either way," David said.

"How's your meal budget holding up?"

"Barely made a dent."

"In that case, let's make one. I believe we have something to celebrate, don't you? And, before you make with the wise cracks, let's agree we both know what I'm talking about."

"Love happens?" he asked.

"It does."

The maître d seated them in a round booth in the reservations-only, limited-seating, fine-dining restaurant. Charley agreed with David's recommendation of *menu a prix fixe* featuring an appetizer, entrée, and dessert. They both selected the prawn and crabmeat cocktail to begin. Charley ordered her steak medium-rare compared to David's rare, and they chose decaffeinated coffee flavored with Bailey's Irish Crème over the dessert trolly.

The more they talked while slowly savoring their sensational selections, including a Meomi cabernet from California and Cloudy Bay chardonnay from New Zealand, the more their minds moved away from "what-ifs" and toward the possibility that despite the unspoken ambiguity in each of their lives, there might be a future for them after all.

The nightclub had a large dance floor, and they waited patiently at their table, nursing soft drinks between slow-dance selections. The music heated up as the evening wore on, and both decided it was time to call it a night. They held hands as they walked, and something stirred inside Charley. For her, it had been an enchanting day and night, one that had awakened a longing she didn't want to surrender on a casino dance floor.

Standing in front of the glitzy bank of elevators, the ache in her heart found its way into an ache in her voice. "I don't want tonight to end like all the others."

He thought he knew, but asked, "What are you saying?"

"I'm saying I don't want to wake up in bed in the morning alone. I want you there beside me."

"Are you forgetting what I told you before you agreed to come along?"

She shook her head.

"My obvious limitation aside, I'm a bit rusty in the overall romance department."

"No rust on you, Mr. Hollywood. Bright and shiny as glitter in sunshine. And you could take a giant step forward and kiss me."

He took her in his arms, and they kissed more tenderly than lustfully.

"Well done," she said, as tears streamed down her face.

He handed her the handkerchief he prided himself always having at the ready. "Thought you might want a bit of touch-up for the cameras."

"Cameras?"

"Elevators in hotels like these have them. For security."

"I should have remembered that from my years with the cops," she said, drying her eyes. "In the morning, I'll ask if they'll burn a copy of the disk to help me remember this moment."

Their reservation had been for separate suites on the same floor. The elevator doors opened, and they stood in the brightly lit hallway.

They reached their suites, one across the hall from the other.

"Yours or mine?" David asked.

"Mine, of course."

"Why *of course?*"

"Two reasons . . . no, three. I asked you. My things are all there. And the way the building faces, we'll get the morning sun in my room." She paused. "Assuming, of course, you don't slip away from me during the night."

"Not a chance."

The last thing Charley remembered David saying before she folded herself into his arms and fell asleep was something about life being easier when life doesn't get in the way.

# 13

# Life Gets In The Way

David's eyes opened to the first light of an oyster-colored sky on their fourth Route 66 day. As it rose ever higher, the morning sun Charley had spoken of the night before began streaming across the two lovers lying on top of the hotel's signature percale bedspread, still wearing clothes they'd donned twenty-four hours earlier. In another hotel, another city.

His stirring and the room ripening with a warm glow awakened her.

For the first time, he noticed her ears weren't pierced. The only jewelry he remembered seeing was the Jerusalem cross she wore every day. And the Cartier watch.

"Good morning. Sleep well?" he asked.

Lying in his embrace, she answered, "Like the innocent child I'm certainly not." She pressed her back against him. "It's been so long since a man held me. Now, I don't ever want to lose the feeling."

"And you'll settle for an incomplete man?"

"There's nothing incomplete about you. At least anything that matters to me."

"Does that mean you could do worse?"

"No. I've done worse. It means I couldn't do better," she answered.

They kissed softly and slowly.

Charley nestled her head against David's chest.

"What day is it? And where are we?"

"It's Wednesday. We're in Tulsa."

"And tonight?"

"Amarillo. It'll be our longest drive so far."

*A few more precious days together. That's all. That's all it can ever be.* "Then much as I hate to say it," she sighed, "we best be getting a move on."

They agreed, as they had each morning, to meet in the lobby for breakfast. David left for his room to shower, change, and pack. When Charley joined him, she told him she wasn't hungry.

Something about her demeanor felt oddly different to David as they walked toward the hotel entrance. It unsettled him, but he chose not to say anything.

Their early rising and skipping breakfast gave David confidence they could complete the long day's journey well before nightfall. Charley remained uncharacteristically quiet and didn't appear interested as the Route 66 scenery he'd been so looking forward to finally began to unfold.

At first, an unchanging landscape on both sides of the uncrowded highway was virtually barren, apart from sagebrush and mesquite patches and the occasional cotton field months away from harvest. David smoothly stretched Sheila's legs as he sped past scattered houses and mobile homes set far back from the interstate and sights he'd never seen before. A tractor-trailer graveyard, a Quonset hut converted to a church, horse motels.

He kept up a running narrative. Mountains off in the distance rising above the landscape. Cloud patterns that looked as if they'd been painted on the sky with wind as a brush. When he failed to lure her into his one-sided conversation, he gave up and quit talking. But he couldn't shake the feeling a different woman was riding with him.

When Charley pressed her fingertips to her temples and groaned slightly, he asked, "Charley, what's wrong?"

"Oh, nothing. I just don't feel like my old self this morning. Came on all of a sudden. It'll pass quickly. Not to worry."

"But I *am* worried."

Charley twisted her shoulders. "I just feel achy all over, and my head hurts a little. I got a wonderful night's sleep in the arms of a man I love, but now I feel like I just finished running a marathon. I know the scenery is beautiful, David, and so are your words. If you let me rest my eyes for a few minutes, I know I'll be fine."

Charley leaned back into the supple-leather headrest and rested her eyes. She awakened an hour later and hugged herself in a vain effort to ward off chills overtaking her.

"Charley, something *is* wrong." He said reassuringly, "I'm going to stop and get help."

When she didn't protest, David knew something was indeed wrong. They'd traveled a hundred and twenty miles and were approaching Oklahoma City. He took the next available exit. Ten minutes later, they were at a hospital emergency room two hundred miles short of their Amarillo destination.

After Charley was hurriedly whisked away, David eyed the admittance documents as though they'd been written in Chinese. He knew her given name. Her age, but not her date of birth. Her cell phone number, but not her home address. He knew nothing of her medical history and would need to call Marla Jo to get Rachel's next-of-kin contact information from Kristi.

More than an hour passed before a tall, slender man in his forties, clad in green, loose-fitting surgical scrubs, appeared. He called David's name. Their hushed conversation took place as they stood in a corner of the waiting room under bright institutional lighting. It began awkwardly. From the scant paperwork answers, the doctor knew David and Charley were not related. A one-minute exchange revealed that David knew nothing about her that could help.

"What I can tell you is it appears to be an infection of some kind. We won't know for several hours, perhaps tomorrow morning, the seriousness—"

"Doctor, how serious *could* it be?"

"Depends. Some bacterial infections can be life-threatening if they reach the kidneys or lungs."

The physician's words were jarring. David's heart pinched his chest, and his breath left him.

"Again, we'll need more time. Just try to make yourself comfortable here or leave a phone number where we can reach you."

Minutes later, David heard his name called again, this time by the woman to whom he'd returned the sparsely-completed forms.

"Mr. Jacobs, you listed yourself as the contact person. Is there no one else?"

David shook his head. "Not right now. I'll try to get in touch with her daughter. As far as I know, she's her only family."

"Then are you willing to sign as the financially responsible person?'

"Yes. Absolutely."

David went outside and sat on a bench in a carefully-maintained courtyard of manicured bushes and flowering plants on the verge of their springtime awakening, a place where patients were occasionally taken for brief fresh-air outings. He needed to talk with someone, and that someone was Mac. He reached for his cell phone, but an incoming call vibrated before he could hit the speed-dial button.

An Oregon number.

David listened to a dispassionate male voice tell him his clinic appointment had been moved ahead, and he now needed to arrive on Saturday. Two days hence.

"We trust this won't be a problem for you."

David pictured a recently hired college graduate, possibly in his first-ever full-time job. He turned to look over his shoulder at the emergency entrance doors, his thoughts solely on Charley. For the second time in ten minutes, he didn't hesitate.

"Sorry, I can't do that. Something's come up. I can't be there that soon."

David heard again that he was being given two days' notice, and if he was unable to accept the change, the queue of other waiting patients would advance, and he'd lose his place in line.

"I'm sure you wouldn't want that to happen," the young man said, trying his best to sound firm and reassuring.

A week ago, Santa Monica and then Oregon might have been an ending for him. But a woman had given him hope for a different outcome. At this moment, he didn't know what or for how long. What he did know was he wasn't leaving without her.

He still argued for his original appointment despite not knowing if he could make it. Unsuccessfully. He asked to speak to a higher authority. The clinic's director came on the line and politely reiterated the message. As he listened, David reasoned that if Charley hadn't taken ill, he'd still have forsaken Oregon without telling her, and would have completed the trip to be with her. He'd figure out the rest of it later.

The call ended.

David walked to his Corvette, which had barely thirteen hundred miles on the odometer, and fired up the GPS, searching for nearby hotels. Indoor valet parking was not a consideration. He no longer cared about the inanimate Sheila's welfare, only about the Sheila so suddenly taken from him.

He selected the hotel nearest to the hospital, made a phone reservation, and returned to the waiting room, only to be told there wouldn't be an update until the following day. And since it wasn't yet known if she was contagious, he wouldn't be allowed to see her before then. He went back to the courtyard bench and called California.

"Mac here."

The familiar voice calmed David more quickly and in a more comforting way than three Knob Creek bourbons downed one right after the other.

"David here. How's that broken ankle coming along?"

"Painfully. And I'm not getting sympathy from anyone."

"The lesson there, I believe, is about acting one's age and not mixing it up with kids your children's age. If you had any, that is. Say, you got anything pressing right now?"

"A date with a stunning would-be starlet fresh off the bus from Kansas City," Mac answered jokingly, "but nothing that can't wait. What's up?"

David talked uninterrupted for the better part of fifteen minutes, telling his friend much of what had happened in his world since they last saw each other a week earlier.

"Well, mate, as soon as you get your Australian butt back here, we have a new screenplay to write. Corvettes. Route 66. Love and desperation among the middle-aged." He paused. "But seriously, what's your best guess about what they'll tell you tomorrow?"

"No idea. My *hope* is what's wrong is minor, and we'll be on our way again soon."

Mac steered the next several minutes of conversation to everything except what he knew had his friend in a frantic state. The call ended with Mac asking David to phone him anytime, day or night, with any updates about Charley.

When he hung up, Mac went to his home office to search online for anything he could find about Seattle's Charley Chaplain.

Twenty-four hours had passed since David had last eaten. After picking at a room service entrée, he felt fatigued but not sleepy. Restlessness ushered him to the hotel bar, where he nursed a bourbon on the rocks and tried to shut out the world around him. He was consumed with mounting fear about Charley's uncertain condition and his Oregon decision. He paid his tab and went outside into the crisp night air. His eyes adjusted to the velvety darkness, and he felt as hollow and empty as the space between the stars above him.

He lowered his eyes, and for the first time in years, David Jacobs said a prayer.

A troubled mind he couldn't quiet led to only a few hours of intermittent sleep before he returned to the hospital at six the following morning. Clutching a large takeout coffee in one hand, he had his wits sufficiently about him to persuade the harried woman at reception he was Charlene Tuell's husband but had forgotten her room number.

He slowly opened the door to a third-floor, single-patient room, and found it lit by a blueish night light in the ceiling. The blinds were open, admitting the first rays of early-morning sun on a partly-cloudy day. He tiptoed his way to the guest chair pushed between the window and the bed. Charley lay sleeping, surrounded by machines to which she was tethered.

He sipped his coffee. *This was supposed to be my fate, not hers.*

David drifted off to sleep, awakened when a fine-featured woman in a pink nurse's uniform entered the room and switched on the lights. With charts under one arm and a stethoscope draped around her neck, she was as surprised to see David as he was to see her.

She pointed her chin in his direction.

"Oh, I don't think you're supposed to be here. In fact, I know you aren't."

David guessed the shapely woman with red hair and an abundance of freckles to be in her early thirties. He rose and took a few steps toward her, and in a hushed voice, pleaded to be allowed to stay.

She remained silent while flipping through the charts.

"I guess it wouldn't hurt for you to stay until the doctor tells you otherwise. It says here she was given a rather strong sedative last night, so she may not wake up for a while."

David's spirits rose with the realization that whatever was afflicting Charley wasn't contagious; otherwise, he'd have been shown the door.

"Am I to assume you're Charlene's husband?"

He hesitated before telling her they were friends driving Route 66 when the illness struck.

"Sounds wonderful. Something I need to do some day. If I can find someone like you to go with me." She saw David's reaction. "And, no, I'm not flirting with you."

With a nod toward Charley, she added playfully, "Though if you weren't spoken for, given half a chance, I might. Got a thing for older men."

A beeper buzzed in her pocket. "They need me down at the nurses' station. Won't be gone long. Oh, by the way, I'm Caroline Warren."

"Nice to meet you, Caroline. I'm the older man David Jacobs. And your patient prefers Charley over Charlene. Decidedly so."

Caroline touched fingers to her eyebrow in a mock salute, smiled, and departed.

David started to walk back to the chair when he heard a weak but familiar voice. "I heard that. Some of it, anyway."

He carefully reached down to take one of Charley's hands in his. "And a *gracious* good morning to you, chaplain. Sleep well?"

"You're always asking me that. I think so." Her eyes open but not focused. "Where am I?"

"*We* are in your hospital room. They wouldn't let me be with you last night, but I snuck in this morning. Didn't want you to be alone."

She squeezed his hand and continued to speak in a soft voice.

"And why am I here?" Before he could answer, a smile parted her lips. "Did you pick another parking lot fight, one I don't remember?"

Charley and David both turned toward the sound of the door opening.

"Caroline, your patient overheard us talking about running away together," David said.

Charley didn't see David's wink; the nurse did.

"Please assure her we have no such intentions," David asked, feigning seriousness.

Caroline entered the give-and-take with the asked-for assurance while checking Charley's vital signs and studying numbers and symbols on the monitors. Charley asked again why she was there and was told she had an infection, one that was responding well to medication.

"The doctor is making his rounds and will be here shortly," Caroline said. "He'll give you all the details, but you should plan on several days until you're back feeling like your old self again. These things can really knock you on your butt sometimes." She paused. "Anything I can do to make you more comfortable?"

Charley slowly shook her head resting against a pillow. "Thank you."

After Caroline left, Charley turned toward David. "You brought me here?"

"Yep. You became sick after we left Tulsa . . . and here we are. In Oklahoma City."

"What day is it?"

"Only Thursday. We left Tulsa yesterday morning."

"Guess I didn't turn out to be the fun Sheila you thought you had. Sorry about that."

"Nothing to be—"

An officious-looking man in the stereotypical trappings of hospital physician attire entered the room in a way that left no doubt, at least in his mind, that he was formidable and someone to be given a full measure of deference. Caroline trailed behind him.

The doctor didn't introduce himself or display even a modicum of decent bedside manner. In only a few minutes, he informed all those gathered that Charley had succumbed to a low-grade bacterial infection that was being treated with antibiotics. If she continued to improve as rapidly as she had thus far, she'd be released in the afternoon.

"Your home is in Seattle, right?" he asked.

"Yes," Charley and David answered in unison.

"May I presume that's where you're headed?" he asked in a voice filled with authority.

Not warming to the attending physician, Charley said, "You may not." She looked at David, then tilted her head toward the man in the starched white coat. "Tell him."

"Not a good idea," the doctor said upon hearing about the Route 66 journey. "In fact, it's a terrible one. Go somewhere you can rest and take the full regimen of medications I'll prescribe. Have someone available if the need arises."

Charley and David looked at each other anxiously. What passed silently between them was the irony that a place built for healing could also be one where dreams go to die. Their trip had ended.

"Doctor, that someone will be me," David said.

The physician shook David's extended hand without interest.

"Excellent," he answered dismissively. "Caroline has more customers for me waiting down the hall. I'll be back this afternoon to sign you out."

"Doctor," Charley said.

With his hand already on the door, he turned. "Yes?"

"Do you have a name?"

"Of course. I'm Doctor Larsen."

"And I'm your patient. I have a name, too. Ms. Tuell. And I have a question. Not about me. About you."

Everyone waited.

"Does your colleague standing behind you, the one taking such good care of me and your other *customers,* also refer to you by your first name as you just did her?"

The physician opened his mouth and started to speak, then turned and left without answering.

Before she followed him out, Caroline smiled, clasped her hands together prayerfully in Charley's direction, and mouthed, "Thank you!"

Charley looked at David, who had slumped into the chair.

"I can tell what you're thinking by the look on your face. Don't worry. If I need to apologize when he comes back, I will."

"Or you can fib and tell him it was the drugs talking, not you."

"Yeah, right." She paused. "You said it's Thursday?"

"All day long."

"What happens now? I mean, when they kick us outta here, what are we going to do?"

"I'm sure a dealership somewhere around here will ship Sheila to Mac in California. I can book us on a flight to Seattle whenever you're ready."

"Let's be optimistic. I wanna go home tomorrow."

"Good as done."

They sat quietly.

"David, now would be as good a time as any to, as that comedian says, 'Git 'er done.'"

David rose and started to leave.

"One thing before you go. My purse still in your car?"

"Hotel room."

"Whatever, but thank you. I insist you use my credit cards to pay for the hospital and my ticket. Yours, too . . . but I know you won't."

"You're right, as always."

She wrinkled her nose.

He responded with a sly grin and asked, "I don't mean to be indelicate, but can you afford all these expenses now that you're retired?"

*If he only knew.*

When Charley filed for a divorce, she just wanted out. She hadn't asked for any proof that she was being treated honestly and fairly and accepted without questioning what Richard's lawyers said she was entitled to. With the stroke of a pen, she signed away her equity interest in their home. The day she moved out, she took only her clothes, books, and personal items. She'd never owned expensive jewelry, and in a symbolic turning-the-page, the day her divorce was granted, she purchased the expensive Cartier watch with a minuscule portion of her settlement. Only later would she come to understand the "ill-gotten gain" assertions of others. Those waiting for her back in Seattle.

Charley smiled at David. "No worries about that. Please bring my wallet back, but leave the purse. We know something in it wouldn't be allowed in here."

"Your Bible? Your shield, perhaps? Your g—"

"On your way. Now!"

Her mind clearing, Charley remembered her Friday deadline. Tomorrow. And whether or not she chose to honor it, she decided there was no way she'd have David drawn into the craziness that awaited her.

He returned in less than an hour. "Done. Just as madam instructed. Where would you like me to put this?"

Charley reached out for her wallet and found her medical insurance cards.

David settled back into the chair.

"You're not done yet. Been thinking while you were gone. Made a new decision and I don't want any argument. Kristi will be the one taking care of me when I get home."

"Because?"

"Despite your chivalrous offer, for which I'm very grateful, it's a woman thing. Just accept that for what it is." She paused. "*And*, most importantly, you're expected in Oregon. That's why you've had us smoking up the road with but a few brief touristy stops. Not a sacrifice I'm going to let you make. We can meet again somewhere after we're both all healed-up."

"Now listen, Charley, we—"

"No, you listen," she said firmly. "I know it's not your kind of music, but this is all putting me to mind of a country song."

"That being?"

"What part of *no* don't you understand*?*"

Charley's adamant stance, while not revealing the truth behind her decision, kept David from being truthful about his change of circumstance. He left to call the airline to change his ticket, and when he returned, he couldn't resist further embellishing his lies. He told her the clinic had called, and he now had to be there on Saturday, which was true. But since he knew he'd been displaced at the clinic, he booked a connecting flight from Portland to Los Angeles that same day. His dream road trip was truly over, and the end of his remaining life's journey grew more and more certain.

"Imagine how all that worked out so nicely," he said, bravely.

David heeded her wish for "Charley time." He kissed her before leaving but didn't go far. In the hospital cafeteria, he honored their Route 66 burger and fries fare one more time. When he returned, he found her more rested and more optimistic.

"Well, my Aussie friend—"

"And lover. Of sorts."

"That, too, and no *sorts* about it. No more talk about that. Anyway, as I was about to say, it appears we might have been playing hooky from life for the past few days, and life caught up with us. Hope you've enjoyed it as much as I have."

"I have. Yesterday, I talked with Mac. I told him about you and our trip, and he's anxious for me to return so we can begin writing the screenplay."

"If you value your life, and I believe you do, you'll tell me that isn't true."

He smiled as he shook his head.

"Good. Now, whatever can we do to fill the time until Caroline's colleague returns?"

David adjusted her pillows. "Now, now, be nice. Remember, he's your ticket out of here."

At that moment, her "ticket" pushed open the door. This time, he managed to be both courteous and professional, gave them the news they'd hoped for, signed some paperwork, and was gone in a matter of minutes.

Caroline stayed behind.

"Mr. Jacobs told me about your Route 66 journey, and now you can't continue." She paused. "I should tell you that by day, I'm a nurse, but nights and weekends, you can find me on the ranch where I grew up. I have something to share. May I?"

She heard "Of course" in unison.

"Okay. Here it is. I've long thought that God puts road apples in our paths. You know what road apples are, don't you?"

Both Charley and David nodded.

"Well, we avoid them when we see them, but if we can't and end up stepping in one, we just need to wipe it off, put a smile on our face, and keep on going."

Caroline's comments put a smile on the faces of both Charley and David, who sat on the edge of Charley's bed, holding her hand.

"So, when the time is right, is there any reason why you two can't begin again in California and head east until you get back here? Doesn't seem like too big or smelly a road apple to me."

*That one road apple pales in comparison to the pile waiting for me,* Charley thought, *unless I decide not to step in that direction.*

"And on that fragrant note," Caroline said, "I'm outta here. But I'll probably see you again before you leave."

David left to make arrangements for Sheila while Charley checked herself out of the hospital and had her prescriptions filled at its pharmacy. He was waiting with a ride-share driver he'd secured. Charley had objected to the hospital policy wheelchair . . . to no avail.

"Watch out for those road apples," Caroline shouted as she waved goodbye.

If Charley noticed the step-down in hotel accommodations, she refrained from mentioning it. They dined quietly on late-afternoon meals at a comfort-food restaurant within walking distance, one recommended by a hotel employee.

After their waitress cleared the table, David asked, "Other than your illness and the trip ending, any regrets about the past week?"

"Well, setting aside those two minor inconveniences, I'd say not meeting you a long, long time ago. I think I would have compared very favorably to the Sheila who abandoned you."

"I can assure you that's the truth. But then you wouldn't have Rachel, would you?"

*I don't have her now.*

"And you. Other than not capturing my heart decades ago, what do you regret?"

149

"I regret the schedule I had us on; that's now been for naught. It cheated us out of enjoying memorable things we simply drove on by."

"Worry not. That had nothing to do with why I came along. Even though I barely knew you, it was then, and is now, all about being with you." *And in a few hours, it'll all be over.*

"I've been thinking," David mused. "Some people say destiny is a matter of chance. Others say it depends on the choices we make. Where do you come down?"

"I think chance takes a back seat to choice anytime, anywhere," she answered.

"I agree. Let's keep up with those right choices until we meet again."

She tearfully nodded.

Back in their room, Charley looked at her watch. "Pill time." She pulled several prescription bottles from her purse, one of which was the strong sedative Caroline had mentioned.

David decided to shower, and when he emerged, he found Charley fast asleep under the bed's covers. It was still early evening, but he wasn't about to leave her alone for even a minute. He moved to the suite's living area and began writing. Longhand, at first, then with his laptop. The words began to flow, beginning with a Prologue.

> *The true value of something is often realized when we no longer have it and want it back. Picture our world without first responders. Suppose every first responder in America took the day off, just for a single day. Callers to 911 would hear a recording asking them to call back in twenty-four hours. Chaos would ensue.*
>
> *First responders are ordinary men and women called upon, at times, to do extraordinary things. Often things they've never done before and*

*may never do again. Many have a sense of being invincible, perhaps an important attribute because if they thought about being injured or killed, they might pull back in dangerous situations and lose their effectiveness. As a result, they bravely run toward the uncertain danger others are fleeing. September 11th. Columbine. Sandy Hook. San Bernardino. Orlando. Mandalay Bay. Marjory Stoneman Douglas High School. The list is tragically long and growing, with no end in sight.*

*It's not just their uniform that separates them from the rest of us. It's their courage. And all too often, they die in their service to us. Let's never think they were just doing their job, doing what they signed on for. That's true, of course. But it diminishes them and the families and fellow officers they leave behind. They gave their lives for others, people they most likely never knew. We should never forget that because it will happen again. And again. And again.*

*And yet, they're taken for granted. Think about what it's like when there's a bad storm and the electricity goes out. If it happens at night, even if it's just for a few minutes, we realize how much we depend on it. But until it's not there, we never think about it. Fortunately, first responders will always be there. For us.*

It had been an exhausting day.

David's last thoughts before falling asleep next to Charley while lying on top of the bed were all about how and when he might orchestrate a reunion after they went their separate ways.

# 14

# *Separate Ways*

The next morning found them returning to the restaurant where they'd had dinner the night before, and to their banter which had flowed so effortlessly over the past seven days.

"Our last meal together . . . for a while," David said. "But it won't be a long while."

*No*, Charley thought, *it will be.*

She stirred her coffee. "David, what's the one thing guaranteed to make you smile?"

"You."

"Too easy. What about before?"

"I guess maybe watching actors speaking my words . . . in the way I'd put them together in my head." He paused. "And you? Before me."

She peered at him over the rim of her cup. "I would say . . . thinking about God's grace in my life."

"That's nice. My turn. I could spend hours talking about your strengths. Is there a weakness you'd be willing to share?"

She kept him dangling for a few moments. "Oreos and cold milk. I confess I'm as addicted as when I was a little girl. You?"

"Well, truth is, there's this enchanting woman I met a few days ago who makes me weak all over just thinking about her. I confess I'm addicted."

An "Oh, please" look, followed by, "Sweet-talked in a restaurant somewhere in Oklahoma by a devilishly handsome Australian I met in a bar in Kentucky on his way home to California. Can it get any better than this?"

"I believe it can. And will."

"Me, too." *What else can I say?* "My turn. What's the one thing guaranteed to make you happy? And don't say me."

"Wasn't going to."

"Yes, you were."

"Yes, I was." He paused. "Easy answer. Time spent with my best friend."

"Tell me about Mac."

"I'd rather talk about you."

Arms folded across her chest, her expression told him the next words would have to be his.

"All right. As good a friend as a man could possibly have. We met soon after I landed in LA from New York. Anxious for the two of you to meet. Okay, now you."

"What makes me happy?"

David nodded.

She clasped her hands together on the edge of the table. "Ice cream."

David rested his elbow on the table and his chin on his closed hand. "Food, again?"

Her turn to nod.

"Rather trivial, don't you think? he asked. "I thought we were being serious."

"I *am* being serious."

"Okay, I'm intrigued. Why?"

"Simple, really. And it's how I want to think about my life when I'm old." It wasn't the first time she saw a "go on" look in his eyes. "It'll be the simple things that matter most. With ice cream, all I'll need is the ability to get it . . . and the means to afford it."

David marveled at her thinking. "I'm gonna keep annoying you. You have a gift. You can begin by helping me with the article. I started on it last night while you were sleeping."

The burden of hiding so much from him itched like a wound that wouldn't heal. And it was too late for the salve of honesty. "I look forward to us annoying each other."

They sat quietly for a time.

"Do you think of yourself as sentimental?" Charley asked.

"Never been big on it, except in what I write. I think people attach too much feeling to things often remembered wrong." David looked at his watch. "And on that sentimental note . . . time to go."

---

A week ago, the Corvette's anatomy constrained them to what now would be carry-on luggage. As soon as they arrived inside the airport, David thought of something and excused himself to go back out curbside to call the dealer with whom he'd entrusted Sheila. Charley seized the opportunity to carefully and discretely stash her gun in a coin-operated combination locker.

His flight to Portland would depart an hour before hers. After passing through security, they walked hand-in-hand to his gate near hers and sat facing the windows, their backs to distracting passengers.

"Hope you don't mind. I spent a little extra on your credit card. Got you upfront. And I thought you might like a window seat on your way in."

Charley looked at her boarding pass. "You needn't have, but that's very kind."

They sat quietly, holding hands, as passengers spilled out of the arriving plane that would soon carry David away. When he left to visit the restroom, she buried her shield deep into the smaller of his two leather bags.

He returned as his flight was being called. "That would be me. One last question."

She lifted her eyebrows.

"Would you be at all opposed to PDA? You know, public display of—"

"I know what it means, in American *and* Australian. Let's get to it."

They kissed, then held each other tightly.

He reached to pick up his luggage. "I'll call you."

"Give me at least a day or two to get settled. And you. You keep your hands to yourself with the nurses where you're going. Especially any that look like Caroline."

He bowed. "Yes ma'am."

Before he queued with the other passengers, David asked if he could enter Mac's number in her phone. "You might need to call him some day."

A final kiss.

She watched the plane push back and taxi out of view.

Feeling all alone in the crowed concourse, Charley knew it was decision time. She'd have to surrender her life in one of two ways. A week's thinking helped her decide to let it happen on her terms.

Soon. Perhaps at a remote location somewhere along Route 66.

She headed toward the main terminal . . . and the locker. But as she walked, an opposing thought crept into her mind. Was her trip-shortening twist of fate some sort of signpost directing her to a courageous return to Seattle to endure whatever fate awaited her?

Her competing thoughts blurred until she remembered something she'd written about contentment in her ex-husband's bestselling book. *"If the voice you hear inside your head is smarter than you know you are, then something else is at work."*

She dropped her bags, sat down, narrowed her eyes in thought, and then uttered aloud, "Signpost."

Her cell phone vibrated in her purse. Caller ID displayed "Kristi."

She caught the call on the sixth ring and heard Kristi scold her for not staying in touch before asking for an update.

Charley told her their road trip had ended far short of their California destination.

"Where are you?" Kristi asked.

"At the airport in Oklahoma City."

"Is David with you?"

"No. He left a little while ago. He needed to be in Oregon tomorrow." She paused. "It's a very long story."

"And one I'm going to make you tell me in excruciating detail. Now, when will that be? Wait! You said you're at an airport. Have you finally come to your senses? Are on your way back home?"

Charley heard the first boarding call for her flight.

"Charley? Are you still there?"

Several seconds of silence. "Yes. I'm on my way back."

As Charley approached her gate, she was astonished to see two familiar faces. They belonged to men so unremarkable no one would ever guess they were among Seattle's best undercover detectives. She knew them well and remembered them fondly. Because of their ill-fitting suits and opposite physiques, others on the force, but never Charley, called them Laurel and Hardy.

They shook hands before Charley said, "There's no way this is a coincidence, is there?"

Both men shook their heads.

The taller, thinner Laurel told Charley the ticket purchase using her credit card had alerted the Seattle police to her whereabouts and travel plans. The stout Hardy explained their respect and affection for her was such that they'd volunteered to fly to Oklahoma City to escort her back and suggested she call her attorney so he could be waiting.

When David arrived in Portland, instead of lounging around waiting three hours for his connecting flight to LA, he decided to use the time to drop by the clinic unannounced to plead his case in person. *Nothing ventured,* he told himself; *nothing gained.* And at a cost of but a few grains of sand in his hourglass of remaining time.

At Karen's Kastle, even before she knew his name, Charley told David all that was left was for them to go their separate ways, back to their separate lives.

# 15

# *Separate Lives*

Charley's attorney was waiting in front of a familiar building. The Seattle Adult Detention Center on Third Avenue in the downtown central business district. She clutched at his arm as they entered and steeled herself for an altogether different experience. Prisoner instead of cop. She'd been audacious in confronting dangerous miscreants in a restaurant parking lot, but as she prepared to be held against her will, behind bars on the inside looking out, she was petrified.

She gave her lawyer her cell phone, Cartier watch, and Jerusalem cross necklace, to pass on to her friend Kristi. At Charley's request, the lawyer gave the authorities the airport locker number and combination, cautioning them it contained a loaded handgun. Within the first hour of in-take processing, she was examined by an on-call physician. She learned at least the first full week of incarceration would occur in the infirmary where her Oklahoma prescriptions would be locked away and doled out by a nurse.

With paperwork, photographing, and fingerprinting complete, she was offered one phone call.

Kristi cried when she heard why Charley hadn't appeared at their designated SeaTac airport meeting spot. After she calmed herself, Kristi offered to call David. Charley's answer was the firmest possible "no."

Later that evening, a guard entered the infirmary and informed Charley she had visitors. She knew any visitation this soon was almost always limited to immediate family and attorneys, so she asked.

"It would appear you have both."

"Must be a mistake."

He gestured toward the door. "Follow me."

They walked briskly down three hallways and through that many locked doors until they reached a small windowless room. The guard instructed her to sit on one side of a metal table bolted to the floor. A minute later, a door on the other side of the room opened, and Charley stared with incredulity . . . at her daughter Rachel, and Rachel's husband, David.

They were allowed to embrace, and the guard departed.

Besieged with emotion, Charley tearfully asked her daughter the obvious question: how had she known?

Sitting opposite Charley with David beside her, Rachel answered, "Kristi called me."

"Without asking me. And you both flew up here from California just to be with me?" asked a disbelieving Charley. "I only arrived a few hours ago."

"I was already here," Rachel answered, "trying to clean up the wreckage of the estate of the late Richard Kersting. I called David when I heard and he caught the first available flight."

"I don't know what to say. I'm speechless."

With tenderness, Rachel replied, "Mother, we've got a lot to talk about and a lot to get behind us. But for now, it's all about you."

"May I?" David asked. His wife nodded. "Charley, we know you've got a wonderful lawyer. We've met with him and certainly don't want to interfere. But I'm a criminal lawyer, too. And a pretty good one, I might say. I'm licensed in both California and Washington, and I'm available to help. If you want."

*If I want?* Charley broke down again and sobbed.

The other David's spur-of-the-moment Oregon airport decision dealt him a winning hand. Upon arrival, he learned there was a clinic opening for him owing to a rare April snowstorm in Utah that stranded the next-in-line patient in a small town over eighty miles from the Salt Lake City airport. Because he was already on the premises, David was allowed to slide right back into his queue position.

Similar to Charley yet worlds apart, David began his own in-take process. It went quickly and smoothly because of all the information in the clinic's files, given he'd already been accepted months earlier. The same young man with whom he'd spoken by phone a few days ago informed him their protocol dictated no cell phone or internet activity by patients during their first three days of testing and evaluation, and that his enabling devices needed to be surrendered.

"You'll get them back on Tuesday," the man informed David.

David gave the man his laptop and was granted another few hours with his phone. After settling in his spartan room, he made the first of several unsuccessful attempts to reach Charley.

"Wonderful to hear your voice," he said after her recorded message. "Told you I'd call. You said give you a day or two, but I couldn't wait. All checked in, just where I told you I'd be. Tag, you're it. Please call me as soon as you get this message because they're gonna take my phone away for a few days. Love you heaps. That's Aussie slang for . . . oh, you know what it means. Bye."

Over the next hour, David left ever-shortening messages. In the next to last one, he informed Charley he hadn't glimpsed any Caroline-like nurses, but should there be any, he assured her of his proper behavior. In the last one, he thanked her for the kryptonite shield and would regard it as a talisman to be returned when they were next together.

Before returning to the front desk to hand over his phone, David called Mac, who listened patiently for several minutes.

"Let you out of my sight for a few days and look what happens. Are you optimistic?"

"About treatment here, or about a life with Charley?"

"Either. Both."

"Honestly, Mac, given what all the other doctors have told me, this is at best a Hail Mary. The clock's gonna run out; just don't know when."

"You're that certain?"

"What I *am* certain of is I want to spend my remaining time with Charley. If she'll have me."

"Not following . . . about the 'if she'll have me' part."

"If you were her, after hearing the truth, would you find me worthy enough to see again?"

"Well, let's first get out of the way that you're not my type."

David smiled for the first time in a couple of days.

"But to answer your question, if she's all that you say she is—"

"She is . . . and more."

"Then yes. She'll want to be with you." Mac turned solemn. "For as long as that might be. But you're right, mate. From what you've shared, you've got a lot of explaining to do. Then, if she doesn't shoot you with that gun of hers, turning on a bit of Aussie charm might not be a bad idea."

Mac's words caused David to recall reading that a person could live a few weeks without food, a few days without water, and a few minutes without oxygen. To that, he drew from his metaphorical bank and added: but only seconds without hope.

He told Mac he had hope for both a favorable treatment outcome, something he didn't really believe, and being with Charley, something he hoped for with all his heart. Before they hung up, David told his friend they couldn't speak again until the coming Tuesday.

Alone that evening, David's thoughts churned recollections of the past week and pathways for unwinding his deception when he and Charley would be together again. Before sleep claimed him, holding her shield in his hand, he recalled her "I've got this" bravery. And for the first time, he wondered what she'd done with the weapon since she'd said nothing further and was at his side when they passed through airport security. His last waking thought was a mental note to ask.

Charley's Seattle attorney and Rachel's David stood on either side of her for her first court appearance. Rachel sat in the gallery behind them, along with reporters who'd been tipped off to a potentially newsworthy encounter on the court's early Monday morning docket. All heard the judge say that because of Richard's flight out of the country and Charley's unlawful leaving the jurisdiction, bail or home detention would be denied but reconsidered at a later date.

Toward the end of the afternoon, Rachel paid her mother a visit in the same room where they'd met on Friday evening. Charley decided against talking about David and their Route 66 journey. Instead, she asked about Rachel's estate settlement work and wasn't one bit surprised to learn her ex-husband had excluded her. Before her daughter left, Charley asked her to meet with Kristi and send her expensive watch to a woman in a small town in Oklahoma.

"She spells her name Sioux-Z and works at a restaurant in Chelsea. I'm sure you can find her."

Rachel turned her head slightly to form a silent question.

"Long story. Another time. But thank you for doing this for me," Charley said.

Rachel began to leave.

"What caused his death?" Charley asked, stopping her daughter. "The illustrious Reverand Kersting."

"Didn't you know?"

Charley shook her head.

"Heart attack. Surprising, isn't it?"

"In what way?" Charley asked.

"Didn't think he had one."

"It certainly withered away to next to nothing over time. Well, if he hadn't died, he'd sure have hell to pay here . . . along with me."

"Don't worry, mother. He'll be paying in hell forever."

A busy weekend schedule caused Mac to shelve his curiosity until late Monday morning when he finished the last of his coffee and moved from the oceanfront deck of his residence near the Santa Monica Pier to his home office. He began an internet search about Seattle's Charley Chaplain and read the early reporting of her courtroom plight. He knew David would have no way of knowing until the next day when his computer and phone were returned.

Late that same Monday afternoon, David answered a soft knock on his door. Surprised would be an understatement as David invited his visitor to "come on in," and a predictable exchange of pleasantries took place between best friends of decades-long standing.

"Might I ask what brings you to this posh retreat?" David asked. When Mac hesitated, David continued. "I can assure you I don't need any hand-holding for the coming festivities, and I further assure you no fetching single nurses are looking for a good time with an over-the-hill Hollywood hack like you."

Mac remained silent.

"So, does your presence here mean you've recently watched "*One Flew Over the Cuckoo Nest*" and masterminded an escape for me and the other asylum inmates?"

Still nothing from Mac.

"Are you here on some kind of mission?" Thinking of Charley's banter of several days ago, David added, "A *secret* mission?"

"Maybe yes, maybe no," Mac finally answered.

Perplexed by his friend's arrival and odd behavior, David replied, "Maybe rain, maybe snow."

"Huh?"

"Something I heard not too long ago in a faraway land. So, Mac, why *are* you here?"

Grief-stricken wouldn't begin to describe David after he read the printouts of online news stories Mac handed him. David tossed the papers onto the bed and told Mac he would fly north as soon as possible to be with the woman he'd so quickly and completely fallen in love with.

"David, I understand. I really do. In your place, I'd be thinking the same way. Maybe. But let's talk about reality, can we?"

David nodded and began removing his limited wardrobe from the closet.

"With all our years together creating conflict among fictional characters, can you think of any scenario for this one other than you telling Charley the truth? And by that I mean the whole truth."

"I was going to do that anyway," David answered, folding his clothes. "This just kicks it forward."

"That it does. And let's think about *that* for a moment. You say you love her, and I have no doubt you do. Is what she doesn't know about your illness something you want to unload on her when she's both sick and facing the possibility of prison for many years?"

David didn't respond.

"Well?"

"All I know is I have to see her. Be with her."

"I understand. Believe me, I do. Do we even know if they'll let you see her if you go up there?"

David shook his head.

"And if you could be with her, which I doubt, think of the cost."

"Money's no object," David answered.

"Of course, it's not. Not thinking of money. I'm talking about the toll on her. And on you. There's too much at stake to pull the plug before your assessment here begins. Let alone the possibility of treatment."

"Still going. Gonna find a way to see her. Be with her. Talk with her."

"And say what?"

Blinded by love and unwilling to give in, David answered, "Lay it all out for her. Hope that she'll understand and forgive me."

"May I tell you what I think?" Mac asked, uncertain how far he could push their friendship.

"Sure."

"Two things. First, the impact on Charley will be the same on the phone or in person. You have to know that. Second, and I'm so hesitant to bring up what is so glaringly obvious, she hasn't been truthful with you. All I know of what you talked about in your time together is what you've shared, but we both know she didn't tell you she was a fugitive or all the rest that goes with it. Is it possible there's a lot more she didn't share? Or that some of the things she did tell you weren't truthful?"

David had finished packing. "Mac, I hear what you're saying. But if I can't see her, be with her, I have to talk with her. That's all there is to it."

Fearful of what that would mean for his friend and his friend's lover, Mac cautiously suggested getting another opinion. A tie-breaker.

"And who do you have in mind?" David asked.

"Someone who knows both of you. I know Charley just met her, but Marla Jo Taylor seems to be the only possible choice."

When Marla Jo answered, David switched to the speaker function on Mac's cell phone. She said "yes," she knew about Charley, and told David she'd left a message on his phone late Saturday night after Kristi called her with the sad news.

"I'm at the clinic in Oregon I told you about. Mac is here with me. Trying to decide what to do."

"What do your instincts tell you?"

"Fly to Seattle to be with her. Mac says I shouldn't. They confiscated my phone, and I won't get it back until Tuesday. I want to call her using his phone; he says I shouldn't. We agreed on you as a tie-breaker."

"Wonderful. Well, David, it's only natural for you to feel that way—"

"That's what Mac told me."

"—but since you asked me, your instincts are all wrong."

Knowing how Charley felt about David, with Mac wisely remaining mute, Marla Jo told David he'd selfishly add to Charley's anguish with something she could do nothing about.

In concert with Mac, Marla Jo urged David to focus on his own health to enable a positive reunion in the future.

"After all," she said, "with what you've told us, you'll know so much more about your own situation in only a few days. And, sadly, Charley isn't going anywhere anytime soon."

David tapped into his bank of analogies and metaphors one more time. He silently rationalized their mutual deceptions, his and Charley's, would not be at all unlike what happened in O. Henry's memorable short story, *The Gift of the Magi,* about two people in love doing something for the other at Christmas. A story that ended in irony.

Before the call ended, David told his friends he would acquiesce to their advice.

Mac stayed with David for a few hours until his flight back to LA that night.

In Seattle, Charley's bail denial remained intact. After a week, the nurse had administered all her medicine, and she'd been cleared for placement in the general population. Her request for a prescription for claustrophobia was granted.

A new tough-on-crime mayor had the jail in a state of over-crowding, so while the former chaplain languished in uncertainty, her cell became a revolving door. Some were friendly; others were horrid and caused her sleepless nights. Bad days outweighed good, and all were steeped in a sense of hopelessness.

After several weeks, a measure of certainty came in the form of a scheduled trial date. Still months away. Toward the end of the year.

Although Charley chose not to discuss with her daughter the week she'd spent with David, she thought of him at least once every waking hour. She regretted so many unasked questions. What makes you laugh? What makes you cry? What are the things you love or have loved the most? What do you fear? What don't you fear? What, if anything, do you envy in others? What causes you the greatest worry? What keeps you from falling asleep at night?

Charley often fell asleep guessing what David's answers might have been. And hers. The wondering breathed a tiny bit of distraction into her otherwise dismal world.

David began the meticulous diagnostic process he'd anticipated. At the end of the first full week, he learned his tumor had changed size and shape since his last MRI, and his cancer had metastasized. The clinic could do nothing for him, either treatment or cure, and they couldn't offer palliative or hospice care for him down his narrowing road ahead. He wasn't in terrible pain or discomfort, so the doctors advised assisted suicide in Oregon was likely out of the question. He flew back to LAX where Mac was waiting.

In the Oklahoma hospital, Charley had quipped that, for a few days, she and David had been able to "play hooky" from life." Their week together had burned bright before it burned out. Life caught up with them.

# 16

## Worlds Apart

David followed developments in Charley's life online and in calls with Marla Jo. He knew her trial was scheduled beyond his anticipated expiration date. He emailed his draft of *Hearts Beneath Their Shields* and research notes to Marla Jo, insisting she honor his promise to Charley and receive her final approval before shopping it around for publication.

At David's urging, Mac kept up his movie studio commitments, leaving David to embark on daily reflective walks on the beach. With ocean sights and sounds as background music, and Mac and Marla Jo's help, he cleared his mind sufficiently to organize the unwinding of his Americanized life.

Charley's memory clung like the scent of smoke after a fire, but his hope of being with her again was gone. He wrote her a letter in care of Marla Jo. By June, he found himself reminiscing about his week with the enchanting Charley Chaplain while he sat in an upper-deck business class seat in a Qantas Airbus A380 winging its way toward the Southern Hemisphere.

Months after David landed in Sydney, Rachel found a trove of documents her father had hidden away that she felt would prove her mother's innocence. It took a couple of weeks for Rachel, her husband, and Charley's Seattle lawyer to compile the documents into a compelling presentation. They submitted it with a formal written court pleading. Two more weeks went by before the presiding judge summoned Charley, her Seattle lawyer, and a government prosecutor to her chambers. She dismissed the indictment against Charley "with prejudice," a final and absolute decision preventing the government from refiling the charges against her in any court in the country.

Rachel and her David were at Charley's side when she was set free. Another two days passed before any reporter learned of the judge's decision and news of Charley's exoneration found its way into print and broadcast media. While friends and supporters rejoiced, her detractors, really those of her husband, lamented the turn of events.

That evening, Kristi Andrews, along with Laurel and Hardy, joined Charley, Rachel, and her husband David for a celebratory dinner at one of Seattle's finest downtown waterfront restaurants. After the first round of drinks and before their meals were served, Charley was reminded she'd become a grandmother early in the new year.

"We're counting on you spending a lot of time with us in California," David said. "Even living with us, if that's something you'd consider."

*A daughter, a son-in-law, a grandchild. The only thing left to make California a fully robust dream come true would be two Davids in my life.*

Kristi asked, "Don't you think it's about time you told them about David?"

Her friend must be a mind-reader, Charley thought.

"Me?" David asked, looking first at Charley and then Rachel.

"Another David. Also Jewish. And Australian. Quite a story, to be sure," Charley replied.

"You certainly have our attention," Rachel said.

"Sorry to disappoint, but right now, I have a phone call to make."

As Charley rose from her chair, Rachel handed her an envelope.

"This came for you some time ago from a lady in Kentucky. I was supposed to pass it on to you. I hate to admit it got stuck in some papers in my briefcase. I'm so sorry."

"No wokkas," Charley replied, dropping the envelope into her purse.

"No what?"

"Part of that story I'll be telling you," Charley answered, smiling.

Charley rushed out of the restaurant to find a quiet place for her call, one she'd been hoping for, praying for, dreaming about. She found an urban park bench that suited her perfectly. Getting a "no longer in service" recording, she dialed the number repeatedly. Distraught, she remembered David had entered his friend Mac's number into her cell phone moments before he boarded his flight. She began a frantic search, then dialed the number.

"Mac here."

"I was trying . . . I mean . . . I'm calling for Jim McKenzie."

"That would be me. Who be you?"

His turn of phrase caught her off guard.

"I be . . . I'm sorry. This is Charlene Tuell."

"Ah, yes. Charley Chaplain. David's told me all about you. Said you might be calling sometime. It's nice to hear your voice."

"He talked about you a lot while we were together. And with great fondness. So, Mac . . . may I call you Mac?"

"Everyone else does. I haven't answered to that other name since I don't know when. Except just a moment ago."

"Mac, I'm desperate to talk with David. His cell phone, the only number I have, is no longer working. Can you help?"

After a pause long enough for Charley to experience heart palpitations, Mac said, "Are you in a comfortable place where we can talk?"

She was in a park with few pedestrians and no traffic noise. But his question alarmed her.

"I am," she answered, hesitantly.

"Charley, I know from talking with David so many times after he returned from his road trip that he'd been far from truthful with you. About his illness. When he heard about your troubles in Seattle, he wanted to leave the clinic even before his testing began. I went there to be with him, and Marla Jo and I both persuaded him it would be ill-advised. He'd squander any hope for improving his health. And unburdening himself, telling you the truth by phone would have only added to *your* burden. He ran out of time." Mac paused. "I hope you'll come to understand."

"I understand. His being here with me would have done neither of us any good. Wait! What do you mean . . . he ran out of time? Where is he? Where's David? What happened to him?"

"While in Oregon, he finished a magazine article he said you inspired and sent it to Marla Jo Taylor. I helped him wind up his part of some things we were working on together before we went to the airport for his flight home. That's where we said our goodbyes."

"Home to Hollywood? Why didn't you go back with him?"

"Sorry. I didn't make myself clear. We weren't in Oregon, and home for him wasn't California."

"Don't tell me! Australia?"

"It's where he wanted to—"

"Oh, my God!" Wetness in her eyes, she almost couldn't utter her next words. "To—"

"I'm afraid so."

Mac heard Charley sobbing and waited for her to regain her composure. Or at least a portion of it.

"When did all this happen?" she asked, her voice trembling

"From what I understand about your trip, David was back in Australia a couple of months after the two of you parted company in Oklahoma. Charley, he wrote you a letter. Didn't you get it?"

Charley reached into her purse to touch the envelope she'd just been given.

# 17

## Closing Act

Charley's eyes slowly moved across the hotel ballroom on that gray afternoon the following February in downtown Seattle. In preparing for this day, she'd wanted her words to be succinct while honorably representing David. After her shaky start a few minutes earlier, she now spoke eloquently with the confidence and practiced ease of a trial lawyer at summation. And the two hundred or so seated in the audience gave her their rapt attention.

She told them how she and David met and how a book idea neither of them wanted had morphed into an award-winning magazine article. She spoke of David's two dreams that melded together—the ownership of what he knew to be America's only true sports car with a journey on what he knew to be America's Highway.

"For health reasons, he needed someone to accompany him. When we met, I was perhaps the least likely candidate. Less than three days later, there we were, on the road together, headed from downtown Chicago to the Santa Monica Pier." She paused. "Things didn't go according to David's plan. I took ill, and sadly, we didn't even make it half the way."

She looked across to a large clock mounted on the opposite wall.

"I promised I'd finish in ten minutes. We're almost there." She took a sip of water from the glass on the podium.

"Some of you may be aware David Jacobs was an award-winning Australian screenwriter with the pen name, Neville Kay."

Several in the audience nodded knowingly.

"David wrote *Hearts Beneath Their Shields* using his real name, and a well-known writer and close friend of his, Marla Jo Taylor, was his editor. She was able to get the article placed in what I understand was record time. It won the award that's the reason we're all here today."

Charley paused to collect herself.

"David chose to return to his home country to live out the remaining time he had left. Because my troubles here so delighted the media, we never saw each other again or even spoke after our trip ended. When I try to recall my so very brief time with David, I feel as if I'm trying to wrap my arms around a ghost, to capture something meaningful that will never come my way again. I know that may sound melodramatic, but so be it."

She felt the room take on a silence as loud as shouting.

"I read somewhere we don't remember the days of our lives, rather moments. Moments in time I shared with David, and those he brought to life in his article about true heroes among us. In my mind, and through his writing, their hearts beat as one beneath their shields. I accept this award in tribute to them and on David's behalf."

A burst of applause replaced the shouting silence.

"Thank you. Thank you so much. That's very kind."

She gathered her notecards as if sorting a deck of playing cards.

"You've all given generously of your time and yourselves this afternoon. Time is a most precious commodity in our lives because once consumed, it's gone forever. For that, and for your patience with me as I've stumbled along, thank you. I hope to meet as many of you as possible at the reception. Please travel safely to wherever you're going tonight, and take with you my gratitude and my very best wishes."

An hour later, the last kind words and well-wishes were spoken, the last hand shaken, the last photograph taken. Marla Jo and Ben Taylor were away on a long-planned cruise, but Kristi Andrews attended both the ceremony and reception. She and Charley agreed to meet in the hotel's bar at seven before having dinner together. The two friends had also planned breakfast for the next morning, each knowing they would be saying their goodbyes.

There had been joy in the Lanneau award event, and Charley cherished being with Kristi and other steadfast friends, but neither was enough to create a blue skies homecoming for Charlene Tuell and Charley Chaplain. The city still held far too many bitter memories time would never erase.

Alone in her suite with a need to disperse remnants of nervous energy, Charley decided against changing into more casual attire and headed to the bar early. She wandered down the hallway to an elevator that, for the first time in her stay, descended the eleven floors to the lobby without once stopping.

*A good omen for an uneventful flight the next afternoon and a new beginning?* she wondered.

# 18

# Charley's New Beginning

Charley entered the taproom and again took notice of its late 1940s décor. Aging red leather chairs, oaken tables. An ornate mirror that ran the full length of a well-worn but highly polished oaken bar with shiny brass fixtures. Dim lighting from two vintage chandeliers enhanced the sense of intimacy in the narrow room.

The dark-haired bartender, wearing a starched white tuxedo shirt, cobalt blue bow tie, and black pleated cummerbund, greeted her with a welcoming smile as she passed six empty stools. She perched herself on the one farthest from the baroque stained-glass partition that blocked her view of the entrance.

"Will your friend be joining you again this evening?"

"You remembered. How nice."

"After more than thirty years standing my post here, it's what I do."

"Well, it's still nice to be remembered. Yes, she's meeting me, but I'm early. I'll have—"

"Bourbon and ginger ale?"

Charley smiled and nodded. She reached into her purse to retrieve the envelope Rachel had given her months earlier. She held it in both hands until her drink arrived, then carefully opened it, and unfolded the undated letter in David's handwriting. With each of countless readings, there'd been fewer tears. She hoped tonight there would finally be none. Before reading the letter, she lifted her glass and tilted it toward the mirror in remembrance of the night they met.

*My dearest Charley.*

*Marla Jo tells me your future remains uncertain, though I'm convinced exoneration is only a matter of time. Hopefully, not too much time. I've asked that this letter be given to you after it happens.*

*When we were together, I often agonized over not being truthful. But there was never a moment when I thought the truth wouldn't be an unfair hardship on you.*

*To balance the fickle scales of destiny, my future has certainty. What's going on inside my head is malignant, and my little doomsday clock is ticking away. Deprived of my first choice, to be with you, the days remaining are few. I've decided to return to Oz to live out my days in the care of Sid and Victor. Remember them? My uncles? Their idea, not mine, but one I gratefully accept. I'll be leaving in a few days. So I had to write.*

*Marla Jo and I finished Hearts Beneath Their Shields, though it's your story, not ours. If she finds a publisher, a contract will be sent to you. I used my real name in the byline, a first for me. It was such a departure from all my other work, and you knew David, not Neville.*

*I don't have time to write a book, but if I did, Love Story and Bridges of Madison County would pale by comparison. I have to settle for memories of those few precious days and hope they'll stay with me until the end. Don't think it's too much for a man in my condition to ask.*

*When the insanity abates, and you're set free, I doubt you'll make Seattle your home. No worries. I deeded mine to you, and Mac is watching over it. You'll find Sheila in the garage with the title in your name.*

*Promise me one thing. Don't give up on love. You don't have to go looking; we certainly weren't. You'll find it again. I know you will. Might even consider letting Mac help you get comfortable behind the wheel of Sheila and see where that takes the two of you. Next to me, he's as good as it gets. And in one very important way, I'm assuming vastly better. Who knows? He may succeed where I failed and persuade you to become a writer again.*

*After giving you my heart, you now have my house, my car, a possible dollar or two in royalties, and maybe even my best friend.*

*Heaps more sand in the bottom of my hourglass than the top, and what's left is falling fast. You may be tempted to find me. In fact, knowing you, I'm certain of it. Please don't. It is what it is.*

*Sid and Victor will take their boat out of the Byron Bay harbor, well north of Sydney, and spread my ashes in the ocean. Maybe you'll think of me when you see an incoming tide on a California beach.*

*I asked Marla Jo to send this letter in the care of your daughter, and I hope it finds you well. Take it from a childless but otherwise fairly worldly Aussie, you deserve to have each other back in your lives. Good on ya. The both of you.*

*I'm at peace. It is my fondest hope you are as well. Or soon and always will be.*

*All my love.*

*David.*

Charley slowly re-folded the letter, slid it into the envelope, and returned it to her purse. No tears. Well and truly within herself, she finished her drink. Several moments passed before she sensed someone standing behind her.

Time away had deepened his Australian accent. "You look a bit lonely over there."

Charley's entire body stiffened. She almost crumpled to the floor before swinging around and launching herself off her perch and into the arms of David Jacobs.

He held her tightly, releasing her only when her shaking subsided. She shut her eyes, then opened them. She took his head in both of her hands and kissed him as if she'd never have another chance.

She took an instinctive step back and smoothed her skirt and jacket to give purpose to her arms and hands as she stood facing a man dressed in casual jeans and a blue open-collared cotton shirt. She lifted a white linen handkerchief from his jacket's breast pocket and dabbed at the moistness invading her eyes. She started to speak, but words wouldn't come. Overcome by the full weight of what had just happened, she burst into tears.

"Charley, I know I've upset you. Surprising you the way I did."

"Ya think!" She knew her lightly applied makeup was now tear-washed and tended to herself more vigorously with the handkerchief. "And mister, you've got a lot of explaining to do!"

"I do?"

She narrowed her puffy eyes and placed her hands on her hips. "Damn right, you do!"

"You're right, I do. I do. How should I begin?"

She steadied herself with one hand on the back of her stool. "Maybe something about you not being dead. Which I had every right to believe."

"So you got my letter?"

184

She touched her purse. "I have it with me. Just finished reading it for the umpteenth time."

"Okay," he mused. "Let's see. I told you about Sid and Victor while we were traveling."

She reached to take his hand in hers. "And in your beautiful letter."

"Didn't come easy . . . saying goodbye." Holding hands with a woman he thought he would never see again, he drew a blank. "Where was I?"

"Sid and Victor."

"Right. They weren't as accepting as I was of what American doctors told me. They insisted we search for a magical cure."

"Did you find one? What am I saying? Of course you did! You're here!"

"Would that it be true."

Charley felt as if she'd just been plunged from the apex of the Ferris wheel at Seattle's Pier 57 down into Elliot Bay below.

"It isn't?"

"Afraid not. The Aussie docs agreed the disease slowed but didn't know why. They were all out of magic potions and lucky charms."

"Did they give you any idea—"

"Time?"

Her chin quivered in silent reply.

"Months. Longer, if I'm lucky. Truth is, they simply don't know and refuse to guess. I respect them for that."

"So it could be a year. Years, maybe?" Her hopeful words washed over both of them.

"Yeah, nah. No way to know. They said if I'm still around three years from now, I may be around a lot longer than that." He paused. "Can we sit?"

As they took their seats, Charley asked, "But why did you leave the care of your uncles and the Australian doctors you respect and come all the way back here?"

David reached into his jacket pocket and withdrew her leather-encased shield. "I thought you might want this back. What with kryptonite being in such short supply these days."

Charley noticed his expensive shoes with no socks before closing her hand around the familiar object. "Thank you." She paused. "David, when we first met, you said coincidence was out of the question. Remember?"

"I do."

"This can't *possibly* be one. You being here, today of all days."

"I talked with Mac often after I was back in Oz. When he told me—"

She interrupted. "Mac told me he and Marla Jo advised you against contacting me."

"At the time, they were right. Anyway, when he told me about the award, I knew I had to come and—"

*The shadow I saw beneath the balcony in the auditorium?* "Wait! You were there?"

"Yeah. My flight from Sydney to LA was delayed several hours. By the time my connecting flight got me here, there were no empty seats. I found a bench in the foyer where I could still hear you."

"Why didn't you come forward after? Or during the reception?"

"It was your day. I assumed Kristi would be there and found someone to introduce me. It was her idea to lure you here so we could meet. She'll be a no-show for the reservation the two of you have at the Italian restaurant across the street. That is, if you'll have dinner with me instead."

Her look said it all. "Your sojourn down under hasn't changed you one bit. Of course, I will."

"Great!" He paused. "You're even more beautiful than I remembered. But as I recall, you were a bit sickly when last I saw you."

"That Aussie charm of yours hasn't lost a *bit* of its sheen. As for me, no worries. Shook off the virus the first week in government housing

186

and shed a few unwanted pounds courtesy of jailhouse cooking."

"What are your plans after tonight?"

"It depends."

"On what?"

"On whether I'm talking with David Jacobs or Neville Kay."

"Because—"

"David lives in the real world. Neville lives in a make-believe world. Right now, I don't know which one I'm in. You've done that to me, and now you need to help me."

"David."

"Okay, then. I understand I now own a home in California. Until ten minutes ago, I was planning to go there tomorrow."

"I hope the home is to your liking."

"I'm sure it will be. With a quite fancy, almost-new car in the garage."

"That, too."

"What about you?"

David looked at his watch. "Hungry?"

He paid the small tab with a generous tip as always. He reached for Charley's hand, and they slowly walked toward the lobby.

"What now?" Charley asked.

"What now?" David repeated.

"Yes. As in where do we go from here?"

"Across the street."

"You know what I mean." She squeezed his hand tightly. "Where do we, you and I, go from here?"

"Let's sit for a moment."

He guided her to a loveseat away from the lobby's center and across from a majestic fireplace.

"Had a seven thousand mile trip over the ocean to think, so I do have one idea."

"I'm listening."

"Remember that nurse talking about road apples and suggesting we finish our trip going west to east back to Oklahoma?

"I do. And I would be totally up for that. If you still want my company, that is."

"More than you can know. But things are much different now. I've lost sight in one eye, and both fatigue and balance are daily struggles. You'll need to take a fair turn behind the wheel."

"I can do that. What then?"

"We make the rest up as we go along."

"Along where?" she asked.

"I guess, for now, *along* can be wherever we decide to go. Though might not be all that long."

"I'm holding out for the three years . . . and more. Many more."

The faint, pleasant smell of alder wood smoke from the crackling fire drifted their way and the muted voices of guests checking in at the front desk carried across the lobby. The last rays of evening sunlight filtered in through louvered shutters in the window behind and above them. Everything about this moment had a dreamlike quality for Charley, like a pirate gazing at an unopened treasure chest.

"David, I have an idea. After we finish that trip, we head south."

"How far south? Mexico?"

"Way south. I think it's time I met Sid and Victor and got to know more about from whence you came."

"Fine by me." He paused, then proceeded cautiously, just as he'd rehearsed on his long flight. "What about me being an incomplete man?"

"Oh, that."

"Yes, *that*. Wouldn't I be something akin to a consolation prize? Like you thought you might be when I asked you to take Mac's place on Route 66."

"You are now, as you were the day we met, the most complete man I could ever hope to know."

"Good to know." He stroked his chin. "By the way, things may have changed."

David expected a puzzled look and was rewarded with one.

"Changed? In what way?"

"The obvious one."

"I totally get that," she answered. "But how?"

"The Aussies docs weaned me off a couple of the drugs the Americans had me on. Didn't think they were helping. And low and behold, one or both were the culprit. And for good measure, they gave me a prescription for pencil lead . . . if you catch my drift."

She smiled, recalling awkwardness during their first dinner back in Kentucky. "Drifting along, as it were. And it all works?"

"Don't know. Haven't tried."

She thought for a moment. A long moment. "Waiting for me?"

He rubbed his thumb across the ring finger of her left hand. "If you'll have me."

He watched and waited.

She felt her heart drumming a rapid beat. "Is that a proposal?"

"In Australia, it would be. I intend for it to be one here."

Everyone in the hotel lobby, and likely those shopping at nearby Pike Place Market, heard Charley's answer.


*FINI*

.

# Author's Notes

If you enjoyed *Charley Chaplain*, please tell others (and me), and consider taking a few minutes to post an Amazon review http://amazon.com/author/larrygildersleeve. Reviews and word-of-mouth recommendations will make a **huge** difference helping other readers find me.

www.gildersleeve.com contains the first three chapters of my other four novels anyone can read before considering a purchase via a direct link to Amazon.

In my life, there was a real Charlie Chaplain, to whom the book is dedicated, and others whose names have been used fictitiously with permission. My Australian friend of over four decades, David Jacobs, lives in Sydney and is the only true Renaissance Man I know. Two fraternity brothers still friends after fifty years are Jim "Mac" Mckenzie and Jim "Jar" Holland. Karen Thurman's life's work www.rainhillrescue.com is the caring for abandoned blind horses. Kristi, who does live in Seattle, is a dear friend of my wife. Nurse Caroline is the sweet granddaughter of my late brother, Kent. FDNY "Lew"

Ernst is my wife's late father, who in real life was a highly decorated career soldier. Marla Jo Taylor is a fictional character who appears in each of my three Parchment Series books and in *Blue by You.*

For information about the profession of my imaginary friend Charley and my real friend Charlie, please look at www.the-police-chaplain-program.org, formed after September 11th.

Thank you so much for joining me on my journey.

With best wishes and kindest regards,

**Larry B. Gildersleeve**

*The Author Guy*

# Acknowledgments

As has been true of all four of my previous novels, *For the Love of Charley Chaplain* would not have been possible without my outstanding editor and writing coach Lynda McDaniel www.lyndamc-danielbooks.com who patiently stayed with me for ten years.

Dr. Cherri Randall entered my writing life with her review and editing of *Blue by You* in 2022. For both "Blue" and "Charley," she provided brilliant insights and suggestions that enabled me to take both stories to places I hadn't envisioned, allowing my imaginary friends and me to go there and take you along. In addition, both the real David Jacobs and Jar's lovely wife, Beverly, thoughtfully and meticulously reviewed the manuscript, providing valuable insights and shining a light for me on errors of both omission and commission.

My new publisher connected me with a marvelous editor north of the border in Canada, Deborah Froese, who was a significant contributor to the second edition re-write of *Blue by You* and the novel you've just read.

I owe a deep debt of gratitude to the wonderful bestselling author Ann Patchett. Several years ago, I heard her speak at an author event in my hometown of Bowling Green, Kentucky, and she both inspired me and gave me the framework for *Charley Chaplain* and crafting every story I anticipate writing.

Cover design and interior formatting by Emma Elzinga.

www.ingramcontent.com/pod-product-compliance
Lightning Source LLC
Chambersburg PA
CBHW051655260626
47170CB00004B/1525